OKLAHOMA GOLD

To Cecial,

Good luck hunting!

Your Friend
Mike L Edwards

OKLAHOMA GOLD

MIKE EDWARDS

Northwest Publishing, Inc.
Salt Lake City, Utah

Oklahoma Gold

For information address: Northwest Publishing, Inc.
6906 South 300 West, Salt Lake City, Utah 84047
ESH 1 23 95
Edited by: G. E. Bloomsburg

PRINTING HISTORY
First Printing 1995

ISBN: 1-56901-330-6

NPI books are published by Northwest Publishing, Incorporated,
6906 South 300 West, Salt Lake City, Utah 84047.
The name "NPI" and the "NPI" logo are trademarks belonging to
Northwest Publishing, Incorporated.

PRINTED IN THE UNITED STATES OF AMERICA.
10 9 8 7 6 5 4 3 2 1

To all my friends of the O.G.B.A.

ONE

As many adventures and dreams began, so did this story of Oklahoma Gold. When two or more cowboys gather round the old campfire, the stories of lost and found gold are told until the wee hours of the night. On such a night, two cowboys sat around a pot of slowly cooking beans.

Lee Roy, a six-foot-one, hundred and ninety pound man, sat stirring the coals around the pot. Mac, an old mountain man, sat across the fire from him.

"You're a'gonna get ashes in them beans if'n you keep a'stirring that fire," quipped Mac.

"Well if'n I lived in a big house and had a cook, I wouldn't have to cook my own beans," replied Lee Roy.

"You'll never get your hands on that kind of money."

"Well, maybe I'll find Coronado's Gold up by Marietta's Crossing."

"Yeah, I hear'd of that too! But you can bet someone's done got it."

"Well, Mac, you might be right, but they had to dig that gold up somewhere."

Mac rubbed his day-old stubble of a beard then looked straight at Lee Roy. "I wonder if there's any gold up around the Oklahoma-Arkansas line?"

"That don't sound right," mused Lee Roy.

"Well, I hear'd tell of some diamonds and coal being dug up."

"Diamonds and coal?"

"Yep."

"What's diamonds and coal got to do with gold?" questioned Lee Roy.

"Wherever you find 'em, you'll find gold," answered Mac.

At this point, Big Bob came riding into camp on a big black horse. "Hey boys, how's the beans?"

"Ah, they're fair to middling—be better if we had some bacon in 'em."

Big Bob picked up a spoon and tasted the beans. "Whoawee! Them's a little hot!"

"Well, we only used four howl-o-penyas."

"Howl-o-penyas is a good name for fire," replied Bob.

"Just right," smiled Lee Roy.

"M'm good," Mac said as he licked his lips.

Big Bob went to his horse and took a drink from his canteen and returned to the camp fire.

"When we sell this herd in the morning to the King Ranch, I'm gonna take my pay and ride as far away from these flatlands as I can go!"

"How do you feel about prospecting for gold in Oklahoma?"

Big Bob looked at the other two and cocked his head. "You boys got a line on something?"

"Ain't nothing for sure, but they're finding diamonds and

coal on the Oklahoma-Arkansas line."

"Diamonds and coal huh?"

"Yep, and you know what that means."

"Sure! Where there's diamonds and coal, there's gold."

"You guys aren't kidding, that's what Mac told me awhile ago," Lee Roy said wide-eyed.

"Tell you boys what, I'll talk to some of the other hands and y'all do the same. We get a few riders that can shoot straight and are willing to work. We ought to be able to hold up out there in Indian Territory," stated Mac.

"What all we gonna need?" asked Lee Roy.

"Shovels, picks, tents, kerosene lamps, lots of ammo for hunting as well as self-defense, plenty of dry goods, and some of them newfangled canned goods," stated Mac.

"Yeah, lots of grub, and whiskey too!"

"Yer right about that, I might get snake-bit."

"Ahho-ahho!" shouted Lee Roy.

"What's the matter Lee Roy?" asked Mac.

"Just a snake bite!"

"I got just the cure in my saddle bags!" Big Bob smiled as he winked at Mac, dragging out a big bottle of cheap whiskey and handing it to Lee Roy.

"I don't know which is worse—the snake poison or the whiskey." Lee Roy frowned as he turned the bottle up and took a big slug.

"Here's to gold," Mac said, taking the bottle from Lee Roy and taking a swallow. Mac offered, the bottle to Bob.

"Here's to a good cook!" Big Bob offered, taking a big drink.

"Here's to a safe journey," added Lee Roy.

The next day, Big Bob, Mac, and Lee Roy drove their herd past the headquarters for the King Ranch. They were welcomed by the ranch foreman and several Mexican hands. It so happened that it was payday on the big ranch, and all the Mexican cowboys were in a good mood. The foreman picked out a fat calf from those brought in by Big Bob, and the Mexicans wasted no time in skinning him and starting a pit fire.

"Say, Big Bob, let's go in the house and have a drink," suggested John.

"Sure, John."

"Those are good young stuff y'all brought in."

"Thanks, John."

"I counted eight hundred and fifty-three head."

"That's my tally," said Big Bob as he raised his glass to have a drink.

"Here's a bank draft for twelve thousand, seven hundred, and ninety-five dollars," John said. He blew the ink dry on the check and handed it to Big Bob.

"Thanks," said Big Bob.

Watching John take another drink, Big Bob put the money in his wallet. Shaking hands on a finished deal, Big Bob and John had a couple more drinks.

Meanwhile, Mac and Lee Roy were busy round the old campfire talking to their Mexican friends about a trip up north. Pancho had been elected to serve as cook on the calf barbeque, and he wasted no time in getting a big fire built while the others cleaned the young beef. Consequently, the barbeque was cooking before Big Bob had even finished his tally of the stock.

"Say, Pancho, ever think about taking off all summer and going fishing and hunting for gold?"

"*Sí Señor* Mac, I've plenty of money and time, but where would we find gold?" asked Pancho.

"Up around the Oklahoma-Arkansas line, they're finding diamonds and coal," Lee Roy chimed in.

"Oh, I see there's already two of you willing to go!" laughed Pancho.

"Actually there's three, counting Big Bob," stated Mac.

Cruz, who had been listening as he stood by the fire, spoke up, "If Big Bob is going, it's a sure bet there'll be some gold or other valuable goods involved before it's over."

"Yeah, he's got the Midas touch," laughed Lee Roy.

"Well, Cruz, if you go along, that will make five."

"If you're crazy enough to throw in with Big Bob, then count me and my brother Emanuel in too," said Cruz, with a smile that lifted the corners of his big black mustache.

"Is it fit to eat yet?" asked Big Bob as he stepped out of the house, heading for the barbeque.

Everybody turned to look at him with funny looks.

"What'd I say wrong?" asked Big Bob.

"Big Bob, Big Bob…" started Pancho, then the others joined in.

"Big Bob! Big Bob! Big Bob!" they chanted.

"What's this all about?" asked Big Bob.

"You've just been chosen as our leader on the gold-hunting expedition," explained Mac.

"All right, all right!" chuckled Big Bob. "You fellas were serious last night."

"You can bet you're last drop of whiskey on it," shouted Lee Roy.

"How much money will we need for supplies, *Señor* Bob?" asked Pancho.

"I think fifty dollars apiece ought to fix us up for about three months," Big Bob said as he whittled a piece of barbeque off the calf.

"I'll do a little hunting for fresh meat," offered Lee Roy.

"We can restock our provisions in Paris, Texas," chimed in Mac.

"We've got a good fighting gamecock we can fight for money along the way," Cruz said with a smile.

"Sure sounds like a plan to me!" laughed Big Bob. "As leader of this expedition, my first order is for everyone to head for town and meet at the saloon for a couple of beers."

"Aye, aye captain," said Lee Roy as he headed for his horse.

"Shore enough," nodded Mac, heading for his mustang.

"See you there," hollered Pancho, mounting his white stallion.

"Where's everybody going?" asked a Mexican named Samuel.

"To the saloon to have a beer," replied Emanuel.

"Well, I'm a'going too!" answered Samuel. Little did he know what a cold beer would get him into.

TWO

Big Bob's head throbbed as he remembered the fun they'd had at the saloon that night. Everyone had been talking about Oklahoma, where there were bears, wolves, panthers, mountain lions, and rattlesnakes—and those were the friendly critters.

Cherokee, Choctaw, Cree, Apache, outlaws, escaped slaves, and crazy hillbillies were the real predators. No one mentioned those. Everyone talked about gold! It seemed one of the Indian tribes had been showing a few more gold nuggets, necklaces, rings, and such than usual.

"Hey Big Bob!" Pancho said, interrupting Bob's reverie of the night. "How are ya feeling?"

"Oh, so-so."

"Y'all remember that drunk Indian that I was talking to in the saloon last night?"

"Yeah."

"He sold me this here gold ring," Pancho said as he held up a large gold ring with a giant *X* inset across the large face.

"That's a right good-looking ring!" Big Bob exclaimed.

"*Sí, Señor* Big Bob. It is supposed to keep away evil spirits."

"Did he have another one?"

"No, this is the only one he had. The redman told me he made it out of only one nugget."

"Only one nugget! Wow! Did he say where?"

"Well, not until the second bottle of whiskey," laughed Pancho.

Then Big Bob joined in, smiling knowingly. The Cherokee still kept slaves after the Civil War and had fought on the side of the South.

"It's somewhere in the Kiamichi mountain range along the Oklahoma-Arkansas line."

"I should have known."

"What should you have known?" asked Lee Roy as he rubbed the sleep out of his eyes.

"Uh, me and Pancho been trying to pinpoint a gold mine in Oklahoma," answered Big Bob.

"Who says there's an existing gold mine?" Mac asked, as he walked up to join the conversation.

"Well, not exactly a gold mine, but a place where the Indians have found a few gold nuggets," replied Big Bob.

"Yeah, and we've got a right fresh lead." Pancho held up his ring for Lee Roy and Mac to examine. As Lee Roy and Mac looked at the ring, Big Bob started to explain.

"Pancho became real good friends with an Indian from Oklahoma last night. Learned where he'd found a large nugget that made Pancho's good spirit ring."

Pancho took the ring off and let it glisten in the sun for all to see. Cruz couldn't stand it any more.

"Lemme see that ring, *amigo*." Cruz looked it over. "The good spirit ring. Heavy, real heavy. Quite a chunk," he added, handing it over to Lee Roy.

"That's something!" exclaimed Mac as he handed it to Samuel. Samuel nodded, and his eyes grew wide with gold fever. He handed it to Emanuel with mock ceremony.

"This is heavy," said Emanuel, rolling it in his hand.

"Well, I'm ready to go look for a bigger nugget!" cried Big Bob as he mounted his horse.

"Yeah, me too!" they said in unison.

"I just remembered old Sam Taylor's a'fixing to retire and he's a'selling his entire store out at real cheap prices," pitched in Mac after he mounted his mustang.

"Well, Lee Roy, you and the rest of the boys head on over to Sam's. Get everything y'all think we'll need in the line of hardware and what canned goods he's got left. Mac and I will ride over to the Lazy P and see if we can buy some horses," ordered Big Bob as he swung his big black's head toward the trail. Mac lit a cigarette as he swung in alongside Big Bob.

"Didn't take you long to take command."

"Well, it's probably a wild-goose chase anyway, but with organization, we'll probably see some different country, have some fun, and who knows, we might get lucky and find some gold," explained Big Bob.

"Sure, and besides, with all the hunting and fishing, it'll be more like a holiday trip."

"Well, sorta," smiled Big Bob.

It didn't take long for Lee Roy and the boys to get mounted and head for town.

"That Big Bob's got us as busy as if it's a big cattle drive or something," commented Samuel.

"You're right about that *amigo*, but Big Bob is the man that can get the gold out of them Oklahoma hills if anyone can," replied Cruz.

"What kind of hardware we gonna need?" asked Lee Roy.

"A few picks. some small shovels, a couple gold pans for testing color," stated Pancho.

"Yeah, I seen some of those used for panning gold at Sam's store. As I recall, weren't no demand for 'em around here. We might pick them up at a good price," said Lee Roy as they pulled into the sight of a ramshackle boarding house.

Clothes hung stiffly on the lines, horses stood stock-still at the hitching post. A fair-skinned woman in her early thirties with black hair loaded a covered wagon with personnel belongings and cooking utensils.

"I'm sorry, Mary," apologized a tall, thin man. "But the bank's left me no other choice. I've got to sell my land as well as this house to settle my debt."

"Yeah, I understand, Homer," Mary said as she threw the last of her belongings in the wagon. She climbed aboard as the cowboys rode by. "Giddy-up." The horses pulled the slack out of the harnesses and took a few steps down the road.

"Where ya headed, Mary?" Lee Roy asked.

"I don't know yet," answered Mary.

"Can you bake apple pie by moonlight and campfire glare?" Lee Roy asked, a plan developing in his mind.

"Y'all better believe it!"

"Can you make Dutch-oven sourdough biscuits?"

"Sure can."

"How's about cooking bacon?"

"My pleasure, is all these questions leading somewhere?"

"Why shore is, Mary."

"Where, for heaven's sake?"

"Well, me and the boys are heading to Oklahoma to look for gold."

"Gold in Oklahoma?"

"Sure thang, Pancho's good spirit ring is made out of one nugget found on the Oklahoma-Arkansas line," Lee Roy proudly stated as the Mexicans rode alongside, nodding their heads in agreement.

"Here, Miss Mary," Pancho said as he handed her his ring.

Mary stopped the horses. "Sure 'nuff?"

"Sure 'nuff! Your old friend Big Bob is ramrodding the trip. Mac and I, along with these cowboys, are the outfit. We're heading to Sam's to buy supplies this very minute."

"Y'all gonna need a cook?"

"Can you bake…"

"Don't start them questions again!" interrupted Mary. "I'll just back my wagon up to Sam's and load it."

"Sure, and if Big Bob don't hire ya as cook, I'll buy the wagon off ya."

"Price might be a little too high for ya," smiled Mary.

"Ha-ha," laughed the cowboys.

The four Mexicans headed their horses around to the front of the store and tied them to the hitching post. Lee Roy headed to the rear door of the store and helped Mary spot the wagon.

"Lemme help ya down."

"Sure. What y'all want me to buy as cook?"

"Well, get enough for five or six months and just use yore own judgment."

"Okay."

The four Mexicans were already looking the store over.

"Say, Lee Roy, come here and look at these picks," Cruz said as he motioned to Lee Roy. "Don't they look small?"

"Yeah, Cruz, they're mining picks."

"I can let you have those for half-price," stated Sam trying to make a sale.

"Well, Sam, would you sell those sledge hammers and shovels at half price too?"

"I will, if it's cash."

"Cash it is."

"Very well. Anything else?"

"How's about these large pans?" asked Pancho as he held two up for Sam to see.

"Sure," replied Sam, then he squinted his eyes. "You boys find some gold?"

"Oh, no sir, Sam, we ain't seen no gold, but we're going to Oklahoma to find some," Lee Roy answered.

"Well, I heard there was some mining going on up there, but mostly some poor deposits of coal. Maybe y'all will get lucky."

Cruz and Pancho started loading the picks, shovels, and other supplies into the front of the wagon as Mary began to make her choices. She wisely picked flour, sugar, hardtack, beans, salt pork, fresh bacon, and coffee all packed in tin drums. Sam was keeping track with pencil and paper.

"What'll we owe ya?" Lee Roy asked.

"Looks like about eighty dollars."

"Here's forty," Cruz said as he handed the money to Lee Roy.

"Here ya go, eighty bucks," Lee Roy said passing the money to Sam.

"Thank y'all, and good luck." Sam waved.

"Thank ya, Sam," called Lee Roy as he and Mary settled into the wagon seat for the trip back to camp.

After they'd gotten out of town, Mary asked, "Are you sure there's gold?"

"Yes ma'am, I'm sure there's gold, but whether are not we'll find it is the big question," smiled Lee Roy.

"What if we don't find any?"

"Well, it beats spending our money on a few days in town on whiskey and women, winding up broke with nothing to show," answered Lee Roy.

"Yeah, that's true enough, but isn't this trip a big gamble?"

"No ma'am, it isn't. There's plenty of water. Wild game is abundant, and we've got enough grub in this here wagon to feed us to Christmas."

"You make it sound like a holiday."

"Why not? Even cowhands need a holiday from time to time, and who knows, we might even find gold."

"Aren't there outlaws and such in Oklahoma?" asked Mary.

"Well, if we run into trouble, I've got this .45 on my hip—a good Spencer .44—plus four Mexicans, Mac, and Big Bob to back me up. You throw something at Cruz and he'll skin it before its heart quits beating. That crafty old mountain man will figure a way around it, and if that don't work, Big Bob will ride straight through it," explained Lee Roy.

"Just the same, I'm keeping my old double-barreled 12-gauge greener loaded with number four buckshot under this wagon seat and my .38 tucked away here in my bosom for fun."

"What are you calling 'for fun'?"

"Same thang you do."

"Aw, quit it, yer giving me goose bumps," teased Lee Roy.

About then they pulled into camp. Big Bob and Mac hadn't made it back yet. Mary got out the big camp pot she'd used so many times before and started cooking beans with salt pork. She let the tailgate of the wagon down to make biscuits on.

"Wonder how Big Bob's gonna feel about Mary?" Cruz asked Lee Roy.

"About the time he eats those fresh biscuits he's gonna feel real good about her."

"Hope he's got us some good horses," commented Pancho.

"*Sí amigo*, they'll make a big difference on the trip up north," nodded Samuel.

"Our finances look pretty good. We weren't out much on our tools and supplies," stated Pancho.

"Look, Cruz, something's bothering your rooster." Emanuel, who had been content to sit by the fire until now, pointed.

There was Cruz's rooster, Popcorn, being attacked by a big black snake. Popcorn had jumped high in his cage and was shuffling as he came down on the snake's head. Cruz was the first on the scene and grabbed the snake by its tail.

"Look, it's already dead," cried Cruz as he swung it in a large circle, then tossed it into the bushes.

"Wow! Old Popcorn can sure hit hard!" exclaimed Pancho.

"He sure can," agreed Emanuel.

"I'd like to see him in a cockfight," commented Lee Roy.

"If there's a chance, you will, my friend," guaranteed Cruz with a smile as they returned to the campfire.

"Say, Mary, what y'all going to charge for cooking?" asked Lee Roy.

"Got a chuck wagon and cook for one share of the gold," Mary stated in a businesslike tone.

"Whoa, hold on there," Big Bob said, coming out from behind the chuck wagon. "What's this about a cook and a chuck wagon?"

"Mary lost her job at the boarding house in town, and I thought it would be a good idea to have her along as cook," Lee Roy spoke up.

"You don't have many ideas, but when you do, they're good-uns!" Big Bob replied.

"Smelled biscuits, huh?" asked Lee Roy.

"Yeah, they smell good, and all you want is one share?" asked Big Bob.

"That's right, Big Bob, one share, and all I do is cook," Mary said, looking at Big Bob and batting her baby blues.

"That's a deal, sweetheart," stated Big Bob.

"My heart ain't sweet, but my loving is," teased Mary.

"I'll be the judge of that," Lee Roy said.

"You'll be the judge of nothing, unless I say so." Mary smiled.

"Sounds good to me," replied Lee Roy.

"How'd the horse trade go?" asked Pancho.

"Well me and Mac, we eased up there like we was looking for a few horses out of remuda. They was resting after the big drive and starting to get a little feisty. One of the horses, a big fifteen-hands-tall buckskin, was showing one of the ranch hands a little more spirit than he was used to. Throwed him onto the corral fence and then stood there like a whipped pup with its head hanging down begging for someone to get on.

"Mac and me eased on down there and started talking horseflesh to the foreman. I believe his name was George, and I says, 'George, them horses is getting mighty feisty.' 'Hi Big Bob, yeah, they been corralled and fed and rested for a few days,' George answered me. 'A lot better treatment than they got on the trail,' I tells him. 'Yeah, they're starting to act like they want to be rode, but we don't have enough cowhands to wear them out,' he says.

"About then, the big buckskin snorted through its nose, as if someone ought to take his saddle and bridle off," Big Bob continued. "Then George, he says to me, 'If I owned that buckskin, I'd shoot him between the eyes!' Then I had my opening. 'Speaking of owning,' I asks him, 'how's about selling me some good horses?' 'How many you need?' he wanted to know. And then he took us over to a corral full of trail-broke broncs that were used in the trail drive.

"'Well, George,' I says, 'I need thirty horses,' He kinda looks at me and says, 'Thirty?' And I says, 'Yep, thirty.' 'Let you have the eight bays, twelve paints, and ten of them duns, and one mustang,' George tells me. Then I ask him, 'How about the big buckskin?' He tells me that if I can ride him, he's mine, and that's all I wanted to hear. Hell, I'd a'rode that buckskin on the drive. He'd pitch a little, then go forward and hunch down with his front foot and kick with his hind legs. After you showed him you could stay on, he'd settle down and be the most spirited cutting horse you'd ever seen.

"So I dismounted the black and tied him to the corral, eased between the corral rails, and walking easy up to the reins, I started talking low and slow to him, like I'd done on the trail drive. Pulled the reins around behind his neck while I eased my left foot into the stirrup and hopped aboard. About then he took off like a .45 caliber bullet. Finishing my mount wasn't easy, and I never did get my right boot into the stirrup.

"That buckskin is sure full of life, he bucked and hopped, turned sideways, then went into his plant and kick routine. Bounced a couple of steps, then turned his head around for a good look at me, straightened up, and trotted over to the corral gate," Big Bob finished sounding out of breath.

"'If I hadn't seen it I wouldn't of believed it!' says old George. 'Tell you what, Big Bob, you take all them horses we talked about for $300?' 'Deal,' I told him, and we shook on it.'"

"You shoulda seen Big Bob on that buckskin, his right knee dug in and the horse just a'jumping," hooted Mac.

"You had more fun today than the law allows, plus made a pretty good horse buy," laughed Pancho.

"Fun? My rear end ain't talking fun!" quipped Big Bob.

"I've got some horse liniment I'll rub where it hurts!" Mary said as she winked up at Bob.

THREE

The glow in the east was just turning from orange to a soft red as Big Bob awoke. Looking around, he saw Mary at the other end of the covered wagon. Her hands were busy slicing bacon. Big Bob drew a deep breath and could smell the biscuits baking.

"Morning, Mary," Big Bob groaned lazily.

"Morning, Big Bob." Mary smiled knowingly.

Big Bob got up and put on his Levi's, his good stout shirt, reached for his old sweat-stained hat, and jammed on his big black boots. Then he stomped over to where he'd hung his gun belt, checked the load in the revolver, eased it back in the holster, and placed the leather safety thong over the hammer.

"There's coffee on," offered Mary.

"Thanks," Big Bob said with a smile. "I believe I'll have a cup."

"Here ya go," Mary said as she passed him a big mug of java.

Big Bob sat down by the campfire. Pancho and Cruz squatted by the fire.

"Which way we going today?" asked Pancho.

"Well, I thought we'd head north toward the Brazos. Hear tell Old Standish got a raft rigged up to cross the river." Big Bob stopped to drink his coffee.

"That suits me and Popcorn," exclaimed Cruz, excited.

"Well, well," mused Big Bob. "I heard tell Old Standish has a few gamecocks."

"Yes sir, he does!" replied Cruz in a flippant tone. "And when we pass through he'll have one less."

"Uh-oh, sounds like Popcorn is gonna get a workout," sighed Pancho.

"A workout? Shoot, I've seen Old Standish's green-legged reds at work. They're tough, game, and they can cut!" answered Big Bob.

"I've got three hundred dollars says Popcorn can whip old man Standish's best red!" Cruz popped off.

"Old Popcorn's been getting plenty of exercise and quite a variety of feeds," answered Pancho.

About this time Lee Roy and Mac eased up to the campfire with their coffee.

"You know, Big Bob, before I went to bragging on Standish's roosters, I believe I'd watch old Popcorn go. I've seen him fight and he is way good," testified Lee Roy.

"Well, when we get to the crossing we might pick up some extra traveling money," laughed Big Bob.

"Breakfast is ready, come and get it!" hollered Mary.

Everybody formed a line, with Mary dishing out a generous portion of biscuits, gravy, and bacon to all. The men sat around on rocks against blackjack oak trees, each pondering the journey which lay ahead. After they'd had a good breakfast, they helped Mary load the wagon and get rolling. Because the chuck wagon was the slowest, it needed to get going first.

Mac and Lee Roy saddled up first because they'd ride point on the trail drive and were good scouts. Looking for the easiest trail for the chuck wagon would speed up their travel time. The other men saddled up and rode at their leisure. Some branched out away from the main group. Watching for deer or turkey, they kept their eyes to the ground, catching any sign. The men rode easy in their saddle, at this pace, which was easier than when they were on trail drive. Whenever one would find something interesting, he would whistle low to the others near him. In this manner they passed the day, making good time.

Cruz had a small pen he had placed in the back of the chuck wagon for his rooster. Popcorn was used to this; he rode in the chuck wagon on the trail drive. Cruz had tied a watering cup on his pen, and Popcorn was very contented as he rode along, crowing from time to time, ever watchful for a hen.

When Mary stopped for the day, Cruz let Popcorn out of his pen. Popcorn would strut, crow, and dance around, cocking his head from one side to the other. Cruz would laugh and throw a few seeds of popcorn out, which was the rooster's favorite feed. That was how Popcorn got his name.

"You reckon he's in shape?" asked Big Bob.

"Watch this," said Cruz as he held out his arm and chucked to the rooster. Popcorn jumped on Cruz's arm and used it for a roost, then crowed loudly. Cruz stroked Popcorn's breast and beckoned for Big Bob to do the same. Big Bob felt the gamecock's breast.

"Oh, he feels good," Big Bob said as he arched his eyebrows.

Cruz let the cock down, and he proceeded to scratch in the horse manure.

"He sure is purty," stated Mary.

"Yeah, an' if he loses, he'll look purty in the stew pot," laughed Big Bob.

"Might be a little tough," quipped Cruz.

"Might be at that," piped Pancho.

"Well, long as I've got ammo we won't have to eat that old rooster," answered Lee Roy, riding into camp, holding up a big bearded turkey.

"Oh that's a nice one," said Mary.

"He'll be good with biscuits, y'all start cleaning him, and I'll build a mesquite fire," stated Big Bob.

"Okay," said Lee Roy as he headed behind the wagon.

"We was checking out a trail about two ridges over with our spy glass. Being kinda quiet like, when all of a sudden, this old gobbler breaks into a strut and lets loose with the biggest gobble you ever heard. Lee Roy grabs his rifle and spies the gobbler about seventy-five yards away in a clearing on a big flat rock. About then the gobbler spies Lee Roy and the rifle barks. We ease up there, and sure enough, the turkey's shot clean through the head," Mac told the group.

"Sounds like a nice shot," agreed Big Bob.

"Well, I just wish I'd seen it," said Pancho.

"Yeah, me to," agreed Cruz.

From the other side of the wagon, Lee Roy hollered, "Aw, it was just a lucky snap shot."

"Sure, and how 'bout the time you shot that big eight-point buck while he was sailing across a ravine. You popped him in the neck so hard that he was dead before he hit the ground. I guess you're just ate up with luck?" chuckled Mac.

"Well, if it comes to luck or skill, I'll take luck every time!" exclaimed Lee Roy.

"Well, luck or skill, it don't matter to me," said Big Bob.

"Yeah, yeah, I know it'll be just as good with biscuits no matter how it was killed," replied Mac.

"Ya got that right," answered Big Bob.

Mary took the dressed turkey and placed him on a spit. Big Bob built a nice fire of mesquite. Mary placed the turkey on two forked limbs and fetched the coffee for the men. Everybody drank coffee, and as usual, the talk turned to gold.

"How much gold does it take to buy a horse ranch?" Pancho asked Big Bob.

"Well, how big a spread do you want?" answered Big Bob.

"Ya think twelve hundred acres would be enough?" asked Pancho.

"Sure," answered Big Bob. "If you run about five hundred head."

"I think I'll have a game fowl ranch," mused Cruz.

"Yeah, and I'll have me a big goldplated Hawken sharp-shooter," Lee Roy thought out loud.

"I think I'll have some turkey and biscuits," said Mary as she gathered the turkey up and placed it on the tailboard of the chuck wagon.

"I think I'm in love," said Big Bob, placing one arm around Mary's waist.

"With me or my cooking?" asked Mary.

"Both," answered Big Bob.

"Hey! Y'all quit messing around and let me taste that turkey I shot," hollered Lee Roy.

"Okay," said Big Bob goodheartedly. "Y'all eat good, 'cause we'll be stopping only once tomorrow, and that will be at old man Standish's place."

After everyone had their fill of turkey and biscuits and the campfire was burning low, Big Bob began to wonder how Popcorn would take the trip, so he ambled off to see Cruz.

"Say, Cruz," hollered Big Bob.

"Yeah, boss," answered Cruz.

"Is there anything we can do special for old Popcorn?" asked Big Bob.

"Sure is, we can cover his scratch pen with cheesecloth to keep him calm."

"Is that all?" asked Big Bob.

"That's about all we can do on the trail. After we get there and he settles down, find him some fruit—it will liven him up," replied Cruz.

"All right. That rooster better win!" grinned Big Bob.

"Oh, he will," answered Cruz.

With that, Big Bob went back to the chuck wagon for the night.

FOUR

As Big Bob broke over the top of a small hill, he realized that what lay below him was prime bottom land. Country like this would make good farmland, or, as Pancho had expressed himself the other night, for a horse ranch. The Brazos River bordered the bottom land on one side, and these hills on the east would make a natural corral.

Big Bob discovered, as he looked to the northwest, that someone had obviously had the same thought. There, where the river was the narrowest, sat a modest rock house. A larger structure sported a fresh coat of red paint. South of the barn were several pens with game fowl inside scratching and crowing loud.

Ahh, crowing loud! That was what Popcorn had done this morning at Mary's breakfast. Cruz had pitched out a handful of popcorn for the hungry gamecock, which he ate hurriedly. Cruz, being in a joyful mood at the condition of his rooster and the thought of a first class opponent such as Mr. Standish, was about to burst with excitement. So to calm down, he told of a certain cocker from Alabama, Nick Arrington, who had challenged General Santa Ana to a main and thrashed him like a stepchild. Popcorn was a descendent of the Alabama cocker's bloodlines.

The men, after hearing of Popcorn's bloodline, began to look at the gamecock with renewed interest. Cruz had fifteen hundred dollars saved back to bet with, and he was going to the hilt. Several of the men had a hundred dollars each to spare, and Pancho was going to bet five hundred dollars himself.

As Big Bob rode on down the hills, his thoughts were on the upcoming cockfight. Big Bob did not look like someone on the trail of gold, which was good, because unthinking secrecy often opens doors that are normally left closed.

Big Bob noticed, as any cowhand would, that the cattle kept here were in unusually good shape, due no doubt to the bottom land's rich soil and the owner's wise choice not to overgraze. The cattle were lively and moved about him, jumping and kicking like deer. Big Bob saw horses on the outside of the cattle herd. They were slick and moved gracefully as horses of good breeding. Easing closer to the horses, he could see they bore the Rocking S brand, the same as the cattle.

If old Mr. Standish was as good at picking roosters and caring for his game fowl, Cruz was going to have a fight on his hands.

"Whoa!" came a voice from nowhere.

Big Bob stopped and turned to stare at a young Mexican man who had stepped from behind a boulder and had a .30-.30 pointed at his chest.

"Planning on stealing cattle?" asked the Mexican.

"No," answered Big Bob flatly.

"Well, what are you doing?" asked the Mexican, his rifle never wavering.

"Scouting ahead for my group," answered Big Bob. Then he explained further, "We have a chuck wagon and thirty horses that need to cross the river."

"Okay." The Mexican lowered his rifle slowly. "Sorry about the .30-.30, but ya never know."

"I understand. A man has to keep an advantage on strangers," replied Big Bob as he eased the hammer down on his hidden pistol.

"My name's Bob Gregory. My friends call me Big Bob." Big Bob smiled, offered his hand.

"I've heard of you, Big Bob, my name is Juan Torres," said the Mexican as they shook hands.

"Tell me, what would be the best route for the chuck wagon to take?" asked Big Bob.

"Well, the way you came over that rise would be the smoothest."

"Thanks for the advice."

"Sure." The Mexican pointed at the bottom land. "This is the best grass in one hundred miles. One night of grazing equals two on the road."

"I don't know if we'll camp near here," stated Big Bob.

"If you want to, you can, 'cause Mr. Standish is fighting a nineteen-cock main against a man named Madicon. There will be plenty of barbeque and beans. Mr. Standish usually allows for extra as plenty people show up to see the fights," the Mexican told him.

"Sounds like a good time."

"Sure is and everybody is welcome."

"Tell me this, how much does Mr. Standish charge to cross the river on his boat?" asked Big Bob.

"A chuck wagon and thirty horses—probably two dollars," answered the Mexican.

"That's reasonable."

They had been riding toward the rock house all this time, and now as they approached the main dwelling, Big Bob could see buckboards, buggies, and lots of saddle horses at the hitching rails. They rode around the west side of the main house, then crossed the front. It was a solid, well-built house with two glass windows, a rarity in this country, which indicated that the owners were well-to-do.

As Big Bob dismounted, he smelled a pleasant odor of barbeque. He and the Mexican sauntered around the east end of the house. There he was greeted by four cowboys tending to some beef.

"Howdy," said one of the cowboys.

"Howdy," said Big Bob.

"You here for the cockfight?" asked a big redheaded cowboy.

"Well, yes and no," said Big Bob. "Me and my bunch are headed to Oklahoma to do some fishing and hunting, but one of the boys has a gamecock."

"Mr. Standish will be pleased to hear that," said Red.

"Say," a medium-sized, black-bearded cowboy said, "did you hear about those Apaches over by Little Rock?"

"No," answered Big Bob.

"They went and bought five hundred rifles and paid in gold!"

"I wonder what they wanted with those rifles?" said Big Bob.

"I heard they just want to hunt with them," said the black-bearded cowboy.

"So far no one's been shot, but I wouldn't mess with them just the same," said Red.

"We'll steer clear of the road around Little Rock," said Big Bob. "Thanks for the warning."

About then a shout went up from the barn as an excited crowd cheered the beginning of the main. Big Bob waved to the cowboys and entered the barn. Mr. Standish had a nice setup with bleachers and an enclosed pit about three feet high and twenty feet long and twenty feet wide: plenty of room for battling cocks.

There were four cock houses set up on the north wall. Each cock house had twelve independent stalls with plenty of cedar shavings for litter in each one. The cock houses looked eight feet wide by eight feet deep, plenty of room for scratch pens.

Scratch pens were what cockers used to limber up their feathered fighters.

On the middle of the cock house was a wooden stand with a set of scales calibrated in pounds and ounces. Here was where the cocks were matched according to weight. Some spectators would let their betting be influenced by an ounce one way or another. Speaking of betting, some of the spectators were making friendly wagers of modest amounts.

"I'll bet twenty on Standish," said a short but stout Mexican called Shorty by his friends.

"I'll call that bet, Shorty," said a blond man named Bill.

"That's just like money in the bank," said Shorty.

"That so?" said Bill. "I got another twenty I'm willing to bet on the Colonel."

A kid about twelve years old stood up in the bleachers and hollered, "I'll call that twenty, Bill."

"You got it, kid."

Then the crowd seemed to quiet as the two opponents stepped out of their prospective cock houses, giving their handlers last minute instructions. The handlers seemed indifferent to their employers as they approached the scales governed by the referee.

The referee watched as each handler weighed his cock. After checking the weights, the referee examined the gaffs. The rules stated that each gaff must be round from socket to point.

The referee then opened the door to the pit, allowing the participants to enter. He took a sledge hammer handle and drew two lines eight feet apart. The two handlers stepped within about four feet of each other and let their cocks bill. The roosters went at each other with quick, sharp movements of their heads and necks. Each maneuvered for the advantage but could not maintain a bill-hold as the handler would use his skill to prevent it.

The crowd had become excited as the cocks billed, and betting increased.

"I'd like to wager another five hundred dollars on my gray," stated Madicon.

"Done," replied Standish as his big red rooster bicycled its green legs in his handler's hands.

"Show 'em twice," commanded the referee.

The two handlers placed their hands under the wings of their gamefowl and permitted their birds to flop, strike, and kick their legs as they showed them twice.

"Cocks ready!" commanded the referee.

Each handler placed his rooster on the lines the referee had drawn earlier.

"Pit 'em," hollered the referee, trying to be heard over the roar of the crowd.

As the fight progressed, so had the spectators' excitement at seeing well-bred gamecocks go at it. Madicon's gray rushed across the pit in a mad dash only to be meet by the red, who had made an equal dash of his own. Their last steps before meeting never took place, as both pounded their wings hard and went airborne. They broke ten feet high and the gray seemed to have the advantage.

They whirled around so fast that the crowd could hardly tell which one was ahead. Of course, they couldn't defy gravity forever and they started down. When they landed on the ground, they wrestled around like a whirlwind. Then it all stopped. The gray hung in the red's head and neck.

"Handle," hollered the referee.

Each handler touched his rooster with care. After pulling them apart, it was apparent that the gray had inflicted just as serious, if not fatal, wounds to the red cock. At this point several spectators jumped to their feet and layed ten to one odds. Some of Standish's ranch hands called a couple of the bets.

The gray's handler placed him on the ground and positioned his body between the cock and the referee. He seemed unhurt. The red, on the other hand, seemed lifeless. Madicon fairly beamed at his rooster's cutting ability. Standish looked as though he had a mouthful of sour grapes.

". . .18, 19, 20; cocks ready," commanded the referee.

Madicon's gray was set down on his mark and made a

beeline for his red opponent. The red had been skillfully set down on his feet by his handler and opened one eye just in time to see the onslaught of the gray, which, in his anticipation of an easy victory, laid a shuffle and hung quickly.

"Handle," commanded the referee.

Standish's handler quickly pulled the cold steel from his cock's head. He had twenty seconds between pittings and blew warm air on the previous head wound. The red seemed to be coming around. His head was upright and he moved his feet.

". . .18, 19, 20; cocks ready," commanded the referee.

The gray charged forward from his mark, expecting an easy victory. The red stepped forward, then took a mad rush at his opponent. The gray seemed surprised that the red was even on his feet. Given this slight advantage by the gray, the red did not hesitate, but moved in for a good body shot at the gray. The red hung both gaffs in the back of the gray and shook with determination. The gray was rattled to death.

"Handle," hollered the referee.

"Damn," said Madicon's handler. "I thought the red was finished."

"He was," said Standish's handler, "but gamecocks have got to be killed."

"Ah! Yes, that's true," sighed Madicon as he handed a thousand dollars to Mr. Standish, who just smiled.

"What will Standish do to that cut-up rooster?" asked Big Bob of a spectator sitting next to him.

"Well, he'll give him a cup of bread and milk, and that poor rooster will be crowing before dawn, ready to top any hen he sees."

"Unbelievable the stamina and nerve that gamecocks have!" exclaimed Big Bob.

"Yes. God gave them traits that he gave no other fowl or animals on this earth," stated the spectator.

"I've got to get back to my friends, so I'll see y'all later." Big Bob waved his hand at the spectators near him as he left the red barn.

Outside he noticed that the Mexican who rode in with him was by himself, tending the barbeque.

"Enjoy the first fight?" the Mexican asked.

"Shore did, and it was a humdinger, a real knock-down, drag-out fight," gossiped Big Bob.

"You going to get your friends?"

"Yeah, I'll see you later, *amigo*." With those last words, Big Bob walked to his buckskin and stepped into the saddle.

FIVE

Big Bob rode about four miles past the ridge which overlooked the Standish place, when he met up with Cruz.

"How's the chuck wagon getting along?" asked Big Bob.

"Well, the wheels were squeaking a little, so when we crossed a small creek I had Mary stop the wagon so them oak wheels could soak up a little water," answered Cruz.

"Well, that's good for now, but when we get to the Standish place we'll have the blacksmith put some good wheels on the old wagon," stated Big Bob.

"*Sí Señor*, we'll also have time to get Popcorn a match against *Señor* Standish," agreed Cruz.

"From what I seen of them Standish roosters you don't want any part of them!" exclaimed Big Bob.

"*Señor* Bob, you see a cockfight today?" asked Cruz.

"Shore did, and what a cockfight it was, especially when Standish's red came back from the dead and whipped Madicon's gray."

"Ahh! Madicon and Standish tying into each other. I'd loved to see that!" said Cruz.

"Well, all you got to do is ride on to the Standish place. The Colonel and Buck are fighting a nineteen-cock main this very moment."

"I'm gone!" hollered Cruz as he rode down the hill toward the Standish place.

About then the other riders and the chuck wagon rounded the hill. Big Bob waved as they spied him. Not one to overwork his horse, he sat in the saddle with one leg over his saddle horn. Big Bob eased out a pack of cigarette papers, pulled out one, and replaced the pack in his shirt pocket. He then crimped the paper and held it with one hand while the other hand pulled a pack of Bull Durham open and dumped the required amount of tobacco into the crimped paper. Then, as only a few cowhands can do, he rolled it with one hand in less than a second. Striking a match, he lit the cigarette and took a puff.

Mary and Lee Roy were riding in the chuck wagon seat together. Mary was laughing at some tall tale of Lee Roy's as they came within earshot of Big Bob.

"Is Ole Standish gonna be able to get us across the Brazos?" asked Lee Roy.

"I don't think he'll be able to tonight," answered Big Bob.

"And why in tarnation not?" asked Mac as his horse stopped alongside the chuck wagon, with Pancho and Samuel close behind.

"Because old man Standish has a nineteen-cock main going on with Madicon, and every Tom, Dick, and Harry within two hundred miles is betting his last hundred on the outcome," answered Big Bob.

"Well, how far along are they?" asked Samuel.

"They had the first fight while I was there, with old man Standish winning. Say, Mary, if you was to hurry this chuck wagon along into Standish's front yard afore night fall, you wouldn't have to cook tonight," stated Big Bob.

"And why's that?" asked Mary.

"Well, when I left there was three calves being barbequed in front of the cockfight," replied Big Bob.

"Wheehaw," cried Mary as she popped the leather reins to the horses' rumps. "Time's a'wasting," she hollered and then waved to Big Bob as the big bay horses stepped along smartly.

After Mary left, Mac angled over to Big Bob. After the horses had settled into an easy walk, matching steps, Mac asked Big Bob, "Ya didn't happen to pick up any information on range conditions ahead?"

"No, Mac, didn't get anything on grass or high water, but I heard that the Apache Indians around Hot Springs were buying suspicious amounts of rifles and ammo," replied Big Bob.

"Perhaps they's expecting to do a lot of hunting," mused Mac.

"Or perhaps they're going on the warpath!" exclaimed Big Bob.

"Could be maybe they're just buying up a stockpile," Mac thought out loud.

"Whatever their reasons, they're paying in gold," stated Big Bob.

Lee Roy had been riding in earshot of this conversation. Clearing his throat, Mac and Big Bob automatically looked his way.

"I never went after anything worthwhile that some amount of danger wasn't involved," stated Lee Roy.

"Well let's keep our eyes and ears open," Big Bob cautiously replied.

"Good idea," agreed Mac.

"Yeah," said Lee Roy.

They were nearing the Standish place when Lee Roy smelled the barbeque.

"Did I hear you say earlier that they was a'having free eats?" asked Lee Roy.

"Shore enough," answered Big Bob.

Mary brought the chuck wagon around the front of the big house and, seeing no other place to stop for all the buggies and wagons, just rolled to a stop and set her brake. Big Bob, Mac, and Lee Roy unhitched the team. One of the cowboys who had talked to Big Bob earlier left the calf over the coals and headed in their direction.

"Howdy again, Big Bob, you almost missed out, but there's plenty to go 'round yet," said Bill.

"Thanks for saving us some, Bill, this here's Mary."

"Howdy Mary."

"Howdy Bill."

"Y'all just dig in and help yoreself. Who ever eats the fastest gets the most!" joked Bill.

Mary and Big Bob proceeded to help themselves to steaming plates of hot barbeque.

They went back to the chuck wagon as the sun slowly sunk in the west, changing from yellow to a soft crimson red. As they were eating, the first stars of the evening began to show in the heavens while the crimson glow in the west faded out. Overcome by nature's beauty, Big Bob and Mary said nothing but looked in each other's eyes. Mary's hand found Big Bob's right and placed it on her left breast. Big Bob's breath became heavy as he leaned over and kissed Mary's burning lips.

Cruz had also helped himself to some barbeque, but had taken a different tack to entertain himself. He watched Mr. Standish and Colonel Madicon fight their cocks to a dramatic tie. With the Colonel winning nine and Standish's winning nine, Cruz thought Mr. Standish were the gamest, but Madicon's were in good shape and cutting well.

When the final match was entering the pit, Cruz could no longer set neutral, as he had all evening, and wagered a modest five hundred dollars bet on Standish's red. There were plenty of takers as everyone was still by and large even for the events.

However, Mr. Standish noticed Cruz and the size of his bet, looked at the rugged Mexican, and smiled a knowing smile.

Colonel Madicon's grays had been tremendous cutters, both in reputation and action in today's main. Everyone had jumped up and bet their last dollar on the outcome of this last fight. The betting was fairly even with the cowhands taking Standish's red.

When the referee shouted, "Pit 'em," the handlers released their birds.

The red cock went straight for the gray. As the gray sidestepped to the right, the red caught him and killed him with the first lick.

"Handle," hollered the referee.

"Mine's dead!" exclaimed the Colonel's handler.

"Not even a scratch," smiled Standish's handler.

"Let me see him," commanded Standish as he examined the bird. He could find nothing wrong. Holding the red cock up, he danced a jig.

"This ole rooster is champion of South Texas!" exclaimed Standish.

"Yes, he is," agreed Colonel Madicon as he paid off his wager.

"He's a fine bird," stated a Scottish spectator.

Cruz collected his bet, and his feathers got a little ruffled from hearing about Standish's red being crowned "Champion of South Texas." He sauntered over to where Mr. Standish was being congratulated by his friends and hands.

"Pardon me, Mr. Standish, but did you say your rooster is the best in the south?" asked Cruz.

"That he is," stated Standish with a mischievous smile.

"I think not," replied Cruz.

Heads turned all around the pit to see who had challenged one such as Mr. Standish. Lee Roy, Mac, Pancho, and Emanuel slowly closed ranks around Cruz as he spoke.

"I think so," replied Standish, "and I am willing to fight any time and any place to prove it."

"How's about here and now?" questioned Cruz.

"Yore on! But I'll not fight my cock for chicken feed!" answered Standish.

"I don't know what chicken feed is where you come from," said Cruz.

"Oh, say, two thousand dollars," replied Standish.

Cruz turned to his buddies, who already had all the money they could spare out of their pockets. Cruz was counting their money when Lee Roy said, "I bet Big Bob wants to get in on this."

"I seen him and Mary chowing down by the chuck wagon earlier," said Mac.

Cruz and Mac left together as Standish waited expectantly. Cruz laid hold of Popcorn's cage as Mac awakened Big Bob.

"Wake up, Big Bob!" says Mac.

"What is it?" said Big Bob sleepily.

"Cruz is fixing to take on Standish's best red rooster." Mac looked at Cruz and Popcorn and smiled as he said, "And not for chicken feed, either."

"We've got twenty-five hundred dollars up," Cruz told him.

"Well, here's another five hundred, y'all go ahead, and me and Mary will be there in a moment," said Big Bob, handing Cruz the money.

"That'll make three thousand dollars," reported Cruz. "I've got to get Popcorn inside to get his eyes used to the candlelight."

Cruz carried Popcorn inside to where there was a good reflection against the wall and set him down.

Mr. Standish was beaming by the pit. "Well?"

"Two thousand dollars would normally be enough, but since we're taking on the champion of South Texas, I thought maybe three thousand dollars and a free ride across the Brazos River if we win would be more fitting," wagered Cruz.

"Well spoken, well spoken. I'll agree to the free ride and three thousand dollars," Standish said, taking the bet.

They both held out their hands and shook on the deal.

Popcorn strutted and crowed in his little scratch pen as Samuel and Cruz took out a pair of two and a half inch full drops midpoints and shined 'em with a rag one last time.

Cruz pulled Popcorn out of his pen and held him sideways

while Samuel heeled him. Everyone stayed to see this hack fight. The betting was ten to eight in favor of Standish. When the two handlers stepped into the pit, the spectators decided they'd stay with a known winner instead of a Mexican newcomer, and the odds become ten to seven. Cruz and Standish were handling, and they began to bill their birds.

"Show 'em twice," commanded the referee.

They held their birds under their wings and let them bill as well as flop their wings twice, returning the cocks to the eight-foot score lines.

"Cocks ready," shouted the referee. "Pit."

Standish's red bailed into Popcorn, driving him into the pit wall with the force of his powerful blows, and hung in Popcorn.

"Handle," shouted the referee.

Both pitters handled. Standish didn't ask for the count, but he figured Popcorn was dead. Cruz felt Popcorn for a swelling wound, but there was none.

"Eighteen, nineteen, twenty. Cocks ready!" commanded the referee. "Pit."

Popcorn drove the red cock into his pit wall to the amazement of the crowd and hung in the red.

"Handle," shouted the referee.

Cruz didn't want the count because he hadn't felt anything wrong with his cock previously, and he wanted to see how bad Standish's was hurt.

"Eighteen, nineteen, twenty. Cocks ready!" commanded the referee. "Pit."

Standish's red drove Popcorn into his pit wall and shuffled on him.

"Handle," shouted the referee.

Standish breathed a sigh of relief. This was more like it.

"Eighteen, nineteen, twenty. Pit!" commanded the referee.

Popcorn tore into the red and drove the red into his wall and laid a tremendous shuffle, then hung.

"Handle," the referee shouted once again.

Standish seemed worried at first, then broke into a grin as nothing was wrong with his bird. Cruz could find nothing wrong with Popcorn.

"Eighteen, nineteen, twenty. Pit," instructed the referee.

The two cocks reached the middle of the pit simultaneously and broke toward the rafters with feathers a'flying in all directions. As the two battle cocks reached the peak of their break, Popcorn maneuvered to one side and hung in Standish's cock's right leg. The cocks careened to the floor of the pit, and as they hit the pit floor Popcorn shuffled and broke Standish's cock's leg. Cruz immediately hollered, "Count me!"

"Handle, back on the count of one, cocks ready?" commanded the referee.

Standish pitted, but the champion of South Texas fell to one side and could only break count by pecking, while Popcorn hit a melee. After the fight was over, Standish asked Cruz what bloodline made up Popcorn's pedigree.

"The famous Alabama cocker who whipped General Santa Ana," replied Cruz.

"Ah, yes, I remember him." Standish, as gracious in defeat as he was excited in victory, reached in his pocket and produced the money owed.

"Do you have another cock to fight?" asked Standish.

"No sir," answered Cruz.

"Would you like to fight Ole Popcorn again?" asked Standish.

"No sir, one fight a night is enough," replied Cruz.

Cruz took Popcorn outside to return him to his scratch pen. Mac and Samuel beamed as they helped Cruz take the full drops off.

"I won another one hundred dollars on the side," smiled Mary. "Ole Popcorn is the best!"

"We had a little luck," grinned Cruz.

"Yes, but we had a good cock," stated Big Bob.

"Whoowee, Popcorn's bad," said Mac.

About this time Lee Roy came walking up carrying a large stone jug. "A Texas ranger from Cameron assures me that this is the best homemade whiskey in nine counties, and I'm inclined to believe him."

"Pass that jug to me," begged Mac as he held out his hand. "I just want one big slug for a victory drink."

He took the jug and held it hillbilly style while it made a clucking noise.

Big Bob rolled his eyes at Mary. "One slug like that apiece and we'll all be drunk," laughed Big Bob.

By this time Cruz had the jug and took a mighty pull. He handed it to Samuel, who made it cluck as long as Mac did. Pancho held out his hand and received the jug, taking a good pull and handing it to Big Bob and Mary.

"I'm going to take one final drink to victory and one for the road." With that, Big Bob clucked the jug till it was almost dry and handed it to Mary, who finished it off. "You're right, Lee Roy, it shore is good whiskey. We've got a long, hard ride ahead of us and I'm turning in. Good night all." With that, Mary grabbed Big Bob's hand, and they headed to the chuck wagon.

Lee Roy looked at his companions and said, "It's probably long and hard anyway!"

Laughing at his joke, they all turned in.

SIX

The next morning Cruz was up early tending to Popcorn when a big, burly, black-headed fellow came up to admire the rooster.

"That's quite a fellow."

"We all think so. He needs a couple of hens. Would *Señor* Standish happen to have any good ones to let out?" replied Cruz.

"Mr. Standish doesn't ordinarily sell hens, but he sure enjoyed that fight y'all gave him so much that he told me if you wanted a couple that he had some warhorse direct from Colonel Bacon that you could have."

Cruz could hardly believe his ears. Colonel Bacon's warhorses were as famous as they were courageous in the pit. Owning two hens from their bloodline would in fact be an honor.

"Let's go look at these hens," answered Cruz.

"Sure."

They walked around to the east side of the house where they found Mr. Standish admiring two hens in a scratch pen for one final time.

"Morning, Cruz."

"Morning, Mr. Standish."

"Morning, Bill."

"Morning, boss."

"I've picked these two hens with their fighting style in mind for yore rooster."

"Yes sir, I'll believe they'll keep ole rooster company and produce number one battle cocks, as well as some fine brood cocks."

"They're yours, *Señor* Cruz, and welcome. Tell me, when do y'all plan on pulling out? I'll personally see you across the river," offered Mr. Standish.

"Well, as soon as we can get our wagon wheels repaired," replied Cruz.

Bill turned his head from the hens and looked at Cruz.

"What's wrong with 'em?"

"The hubs are worn out, the rims are shot, and some of the spokes are broke," answered Cruz.

"Well, normally it takes me a couple days to repair them, but luckily for y'all, I've got four fresh rebuilt ones in the barn," stated Bill.

"Okay, and thanks, I'll take these hens over to introduce them to Popcorn."

When Cruz placed one of the hens in the scratch pen with Popcorn, he promptly topped her, then crowed loudly. Big Bob came from around the wagon and asked Cruz, "What's all the racket about?"

"Ole Popcorn just topped his new girlfriend," answered Cruz.

"Cock-a-doodle-do!" crowed Big Bob. "I just topped my old girlfriend too."

"Ha-ha. Say, Big Bob, I don't think we can get these old

wagon wheels fixed. They're in pretty bad shape," stated Cruz.

"I agree, but where we gonna get some more?"

"Bill the blacksmith has four for sale over by the barn."

"How much?" asked Big Bob.

"He wants five dollars apiece," replied Cruz.

"That's a little high, but we're a long ways from anywhere else. Tell Bill we'll buy 'em," stated Big Bob.

"*Sí Señor* Big Bob," answered Cruz.

"Mary! Mary! You up yet?" Big Bob poked his head in the wagon, just as Mary fastened the last button on her blouse.

"Yes, I'm up and moving pretty good for an old hen!" remarked Mary.

"Ah yeah, only kidding. Say, let's pull this ole wagon over to the barn yonder, an' get her some new shoes," said Big Bob.

Mary mounted the wagon seat as Mac and Lee Roy finished harnessing the horses. Mary popped the reins, and the horses stepped lively toward the barn. They pulled up to be greeted by a grinning blacksmith. He had a pole and large metal wedge. Placing the metal wedge under the axle, Mac, Lee Roy, and Cruz used their weight to lift the wagon. Big Bob, Emanuel, and Pancho watched as the blacksmith quickly and expertly removed the hub and replaced the wheel.

In about twenty minutes the wagon was ready to roll. The blacksmith was wiping away his sweat as Big Bob paid him twenty dollars.

"Never did hear what y'all are doing up this way?" questioned Bill.

"Oh, we're headed to eastern Oklahoma to do a little prospecting," answered Big Bob.

"Yeah, well some Apaches has taken refuge in that area. And I hear that some people are going into the forest and not coming out again," said Bill.

"Thanks for the information, but I understand that it is only one small band," replied Big Bob.

"There's no such thang as a small band of Apache," stated Bill.

"Well, odds are we'll never see them," answered Big Bob.

"Yeah, you're probably right, but forewarned is fore-armed."

"Thanks for the wheels."

"Yer welcome," grinned Bill.

"Adios *amigo*." With that last salutation, Big Bob mounted his buckskin, who promptly started the daily routine of bucking, pitching, and sidestepping trying to throw its rider.

Mac sat his favorite mount, a tough little mustang only thirteen and a half hands high. Lee Roy sat his blaze-faced dun, outwardly calm, but one look at his eyes revealed that inside he was laughing. Pancho had an ear to ear grin as he sat his stallion. Cruz and Emanuel were racing toward the dock.

"That's quite a horse," called Mr. Standish from the ferry. "I'll give ya hundred dollars for him."

"No way! Stumpy and I have punched some mighty ornery longhorns, and I ain't gonna sell him just 'cause he likes to crow-hop a little every morning," answered Big Bob.

With that last comment, Stumpy gave an extra hard hop which landed Big Bob behind the saddle. Satisfied that he would not be taken for granted, Stumpy turned his head around while standing stock-still and stared for what seemed an eternity at the empty saddle, then at Big Bob.

Everyone, including Mr. Standish, was caught off guard by the big buckskin. As soon as everyone had a moment to recover from their surprise, they all burst out in uncontrollable laughter.

Mary was bringing her chuck wagon down the grassy road and looked at Big Bob as she passed. "Thought I gave you a dirty look the other day when you eyeballed that redhead, but Stumpy's got me beat all to thunder." Laughter broke out all over again.

Mr. Standish's barge was typical of the frontier, lashed together with rope and made of huge logs. He loaded the four cowboys and made for the north bank. The cowboys were still joking and laughing when they landed on the other side.

Mr. Standish came back to get Big Bob, Cruz, and Mary.

Popcorn was crowing when Mr. Standish pulled the barge up to the bank of the Brazos River.

"Darn my time, but that rooster is crowing loud," stated Mr. Standish.

"Well he ought to be. This horse ain't near throwed him off and he ain't being laughed at by his woman," replied Big Bob.

"Now! Now! Poor Big Bob," mocked Mr. Standish as he offered Big Bob a drink.

Big Bob accepted the drink, then asked, "Where is the shortest, safest route to Broken Bow?"

"Well, Big Bob, you keep heading north, cross the Trinity River, a bunch of creeks, and if it don't rain, you might even cross the Red River at Manchester. If you're low on supplies by then, Idabel is just across the river," Mr Standish said, gesturing his arms in various directions.

SEVEN

With the new wagon wheels, the chuck wagon was easier to pull, and the group made good time. Lee Roy had shot a couple of deer and Cruz's hens had started to lay. Mac had shot a wild hog, and the deer and hog sausage was excellent. However, by the time they reached the Red River, weevils had gotten into the flour. Lee Roy, Pancho, and Emanuel volunteered to cross the Red River and ride into Idabel for more.

"The old Red's a little low, but shore is muddy on bottom," stated Lee Roy as the two Mexicans alongside nodded in agreement.

Pancho's white horse looked funny when they got to the other side, with red mud splashed in large splotches.

"Ha-ha, is that a paint or a catfish with four legs?" Lee Roy asked.

"Well, *Señor,* it used to be a horse, but now I don't know," answered Pancho.

"There's one way to find out," said Lee Roy.

"How's that?" asked Pancho.

"Perhaps a small race from this bank to that boulder over there." Lee Roy pointed to a boulder about three hundred yards off. "Perhaps Pancho would bet twenty dollars on this race?" asked Lee Roy.

"Perhaps," answered Pancho.

With the last syllable, Lee Roy spurred his horse into full speed, as did Pancho. Not to be left behind, Emanuel spurred his paint into full gallop also.

Lee Roy, in the lead, shouted back to Pancho, "Better spur that catfish."

Lee Roy's dun was fast, but Pancho's white stallion was gaining ground. Emanuel's paint was two lengths behind Pancho's when the stallion's head passed the dun's tail with only a hundred yards to go.

The race was getting closer, and Lee Roy and Pancho both became engrossed in it. They were going hell-bent for leather when they first saw a large oak tree that had been overturned by some force of nature. Lee Roy veered to one side of the giant tree's roots, thus giving Pancho an opportunity to gain a stride as they rounded the fallen tree. Both horses were running neck and neck as they approached the boulder. Horses and riders were very excited as they crossed the finish line in a dead heat.

"Whoa, that was fun," said Lee Roy.

"*Sí Amigo!*" said Pancho. "Here comes Emanuel on his catfish!"

"No, no, Pancho's stallion is the catfish!" replied Emanuel.

"No, No, Emanuel's paint is the slowest, so he is the catfish," teased Pancho.

"*Sí Señor*, the paint is a little slow, but he is sure footed as a Kentucky mule," replied Emanuel.

"From this moment on he shall be known as Catfish, and

as his godfather I'll buy the first beer when we get to Idabel," stated Lee Roy.

They rested no longer, but resumed their travel toward Idabel. Meanwhile Big Bob, Mary, Mac, and Cruz had decided to take the chuck wagon across the Red River. Mary sat on the chuck wagon bench with the reins in her hands.

Mac and Big Bob were in the water helping the horses and Cruz was around the rear of the wagon pushing. They had crossed most of the river when seven masked men on horses rode out to meet them. Their horses splashing water, they rapidly encircled the wagon, before the men could get out of the water to get their weapons.

However, Mary had a double-barreled shotgun under the wagon seat, and she had dropped the reins and grabbed the shotgun when she first saw them.

"Drop that shotgun, ma'am, and no one will have to get hurt."

Mary had both hammers back and both barrels pointed at the fellow who had spoke. The outlaws were pretty confident as they had the drop on the men in the water and only a woman in the chuck wagon seat.

Mary was thinking only two men on her right were pointing their pistols at her and one on her left. Left, out of the corner of her eye, she could see a tree limb floating toward the left outlaw, about then she could feel Cruz's weight slightly move the wagon, and she knew he had successfully evaded the outlaws.

However, the four in front of the horses would soon be able to detect Cruz in the wagon if he didn't move slowly. Too many things were happening at once, something would have to give.

"Come on, lady, either lay that cannon down or use it!" commanded the gang leader.

About then the tree limb struck the outlaw's horse on the left, spooking his horse and throwing him into the river. Momentarily distracted, the outlaws on the right looked away. Mary's trigger finger had a mind all its own as she fired the first barrel of number four buckshot into the upper torso of the outlaw gang's leader.

Enough pellets on the outer edge of the pattern hit his buddy to make him fall off his horse. The outlaws watched their friend fall into the river, then their leader died and they came to their senses. Mary swung the shotgun around, and at thirty feet her pattern was large enough to kill one outlaw and wound two others.

The last outlaw's horse reared up, but when he came down Mary had pulled her pistol from her bosom, and she fired as the outlaw's horse's front hooves found bottom. A direct hit right between the eyes!

About then the first outlaw, whose horse had been spooked by the tree limb, stood up in the water and went for his second pistol.

Mary had cocked her pistol again and was looking for a target, when she saw him going for his second pistol. Quickly aiming from her steady wagon seat, she shot the pistol, hitting the luckless outlaw above his left eye.

When the pistol recoiled, she cocked it again. The two outlaws left up front had been wounded by the shotgun, but were struggling to regain their balance. The one on the right was hurt worse, but the one on the left could barely hold his pistol. Pointing it toward Mary was the wrong thing to do. She let him have it right above the left ear.

The other one had regained his balance and was preparing to shoot Mary when a shot rang out by her right ear. Cruz had managed to find his .45 pistol and finished the villain with one shot.

Immediately, everything was still except for the floating bodies and stirring horses. Big Bob and Mac had been caught under the fire, pointing to targets as they had shown themselves. It happened so fast that no one had a chance to get ready, except Mary, and she had done her part!

Big Bob and Mac crawled over the wagon tongue and into the wagon seat, resting there.

"Are you hurt?" Big Bob finally broke the silence.

"No, but my ear is ringing," answered Mary.

"I'm sorry, Mary, but it was the best I could do," apologized Cruz.

"I understand," said Mary as she reached over and gave Cruz a big kiss.

"Cruz, you sit up there with Mary. Mac and me will gather their bodies and horses," Big Bob said as he regained his objectivity. "There might be some friends about of these hombres, so let's move it."

Mac, an old hand at gunfights, had already thrown one body on a horse and was leading it to another. Big Bob caught the horse nearest him, grabbed a floating body, and threw it on the saddle. Leading the horses, they quickly repeated this procedure until they had all the bodies loaded.

"Mac, you see that crack between those two large boulders?" asked Big Bob.

"Yeah, Big Bob, looks like a good spot," answered Mac.

They headed over to the nearest boulder and peered down into the crack.

"Looks like we ain't the first ones to use this place for a burial ground," stated Big Bob.

"Yeah, I'd bet there's plenty of honest folks down there, and these are probably the outlaws that put 'em there," Mac said as he unloaded the first one.

When they were done, Mac and Big Bob headed back to where the wagon was still stuck. After they got there, they tied their lariat ropes to saddle horns on the captured horses. This gave more than enough power to pull the chuck wagon out of the Red River and into a place they called Indian Territory.

EIGHT

Seven miles down the road, Pancho, Emanuel, and Lee Roy came riding up.

"We got the flour, some beans, and a bottle of whiskey."

"Yeah, thanks," said Mary with her head down.

"What's the matter?"

"We was dry-gulched crossing the Red River by seven outlaws. Mary killed six, and Cruz killed one in the luckiest gunfight I ever saw," drawled Mac.

"Go on."

"Well, they had us surrounded in the water when a tree limb spooked one of their horses, giving Mary the opportunity to let 'em have it with the old scatter gun. Then she finished them off with her squirrel pistol," explained Mac as he patted Mary on the back. "Would of got all seven, but Cruz managed to get in the wagon and shoot the last one."

"Atta boy, Cruz," Lee Roy said as he looked at Big Bob. "The saloon keeper in Idabel said we should watch out for an outlaw gang with six or seven members."

"Well, me and Mac done give 'em a burial. We've got seven extra horses," explained Big Bob.

"We can trade 'em off for pack mules," said Lee Roy.

"Yeah, but they might have friends in Idabel, maybe we'll find some mules in Broken Bow," said Big Bob.

"Sounds like a good plan to me," agreed Mac.

Mary, in the meantime, was building a small fire. She hadn't recovered from the shooting and was trying to calm herself with the familiar work of cooking. The men were quiet around her as they understood what it was like to kill another man, even in a heated battle. One thing they all agreed on was that Mary was one to ride the river with.

Two days later they crossed Little River; ten miles further north they camped on Dan Preston's place. Dan had as fine a mule as anyone could breed.

"Howdy, my name's Bob, friends just call me Big Bob."

"Howdy, my name's Dan Preston, friends call me Dan."

"Okay. Dan, this here's Mac, Lee Roy, Pancho, Cruz, and Emanuel," said Big Bob as he pointed his finger at each friend around the campfire. They all nodded their heads in turn with Big Bob's finger. Some were smoking, others were drinking coffee, and all were watching the fire burn down.

"How's yore stock holding up?" inquired Dan, thinking of a possible trade.

"Well we've not pushed 'em too hard and they're holding fine."

"Y'all plan on heading north into the mountains?"

"Yes, we're going into the Kiamichi Mountains to prospect for gold."

"I've heard tell of a few claims, but none that had enough volume to pay a day's work. Your horses will be practically useless on the rocks and steep grades."

"Yes, that's why we came to you. Your mules are said to

be the best for hundreds of miles around."

"Thanks, but right now the demand is for horses in this area."

"Well, we've got some for trade."

"How many?"

"We've got ten horses left from our trip up here, seven we picked up down by the river, and four we use on the chuck wagon team. So that's twenty-one horses," counted Big Bob.

Dan's eyes narrowed when Big Bob mentioned seven horses picked up down by the river. Dan, smiling, had a good idea of what had happened.

"We're a pretty long ways from what you might call the law around here." His eyes looked straight at Big Bob. "So anyone steals from or kills someone, justice is usually settled out by his friends. Those ole boys down by the river are the sorriest outlaws. I traded with them a time or two, but had trouble. They traded horses that were always tired and wore out from not receiving proper care. No one could put the finger on them for stealing or such around here, but they looked mighty suspicious."

"Well, don't worry no more, Dan, those hombres down by the river took a fatal swim," laughed Big Bob. "And we've even got seven saddles to trade for packs."

"All right," Dan laughed. "I'm so proud of you boys that I'm gonna put packs on each and every mule you trade for— sort of my civic duty to reward you for killing those varmints. Tell you what, I'm gonna give y'all a piece of advice. Those Kiamichi Mountains are pretty steep, and that chuck wagon will be more trouble than its worth. I'll trade you five mules for the wagon. That will be thirty-five mules for the horses, saddles, and wagon."

"That's good, Dan, but we need forty mules," said Big Bob.

"I can only go thirty-five on the trade," said Dan.

"How much cash for five mules?" asked Big Bob.

"I usually get fifty dollars."

"Then two hundred an fifty dollars and trade for forty mules?" asked Big Bob.

"Done."

"Y'all come over in the morning and well make the trade."

Big Bob rose from the campfire and shook Dan's hand on the deal.

"Well, I've got to get to the house and catch some shut-eye. Good night all," replied Dan.

When Dan left, Mary snuggled up to Big Bob and asked, "Where am I going to sleep when the wagon's gone?"

"Under God's beautiful star-lit sky, honey."

"Well, I'd like God's beautiful wagon canvas over my bed one more night, so let's go to bed early."

"Your wish is my command," smiled Big Bob as he headed for the wagon.

The others sat around the campfire visiting with one another. They were proud that they had Big Bob for a friend and a leader, and they were happy that they would finally be in the mountains hunting for gold.

Mac looked across the campfire at the others for a while, then said, "Well, men, we've all been in the mountains before, and we know how tough the terrain, snakes, and wild cats can be. Ole Big Bob has done the right thang trading the chuck wagon for mules."

"*Sí Señor* Mac, the mules will be easier to get through the pine trees and across the creeks."

"Well said, Emanuel! Well said. The mules will not be as scared of the varmints and much more sure-footed on the mountain rocks," said Lee Roy.

"*Sí, Señor* Lee Roy, but Popcorn is going to have to ride on my mule with me," replied Cruz.

"Sure, Cruz, the rooster furnished the money to buy these mules. If'n he wants a mule to himself that will be all right too!" laughed Lee Roy.

With that last remark, there was laughter all around. It also was the end of the chat, as they all turned in for the night. Cruz put a sheet over Popcorn's scratch pen.

"Good night ole fellow."

"Ert, ert, err, errr."

The next morning, Big Bob was up early as many things had to be done: selection of the mules, packing the supplies, moving the trade stock, and hitting the trail. These things were on Big Bob's mind as he saddled up, stepped into the stirrups, and slid easily into the saddle. Big Bob should have had his mind on Stumpy, because Stumpy had his mind on Big Bob.

As soon as Big Bob's butt hit the saddle, Stumpy started his morning ritual of defiance. Big Bob, being caught off guard, was not in the mood for this business and tried unsuccessfully to pull Stumpy's head back. Stumpy reared up on his hind legs and pitched forward a couple of times. Big Bob somehow landed behind the saddle again and Stumpy turned his head and pursed his lips at Big Bob.

Trader Dan was standing by his corrals and went from an ear to ear grin to outright laughter. Big Bob eased back into the saddle and rode over to Dan's corral.

"Morning, Dan."

"Morning, Big Bob, that buckskin's a little high-spirited ain't he?"

"Shore is, but he's also the best cutting horse I've ever had the pleasure to ride. After his morning workout he never shies from anything and is one of the smartest horses I ever seen. I've even shot deer using his saddle for a rest."

"Good steady horse, you might need such a horse where you're going," stated Dan.

"Yeah, Pancho's got a huge gold nugget ring made from gold some where up around the headwaters of the Kiamichi River," says Big Bob.

"Hmmm, first I've heard of gold up around there. Quite a few Indians up there, though. It's Choctaw area but a few Apache move through from time to time," warned Dan.

"Yeah, I've had to deal with Apache before, and they're plenty tough," replied Big Bob.

"To say the least." With this last statement, Dan began to make himself a smoke. Big Bob did, too.

"Which horses you gonna keep?" asked Dan.

"Well, I think Stumpy, my black, Lee Roy's dun. Mac will

probably want his Mustang, it might be good as a mule in the mountains. Pancho will probably want his white stallion, Cruz has a good buckskin, Emanuel will want to bring "Catfish," and Mary will want to ride a broad-backed mule if I know her. So that will leave about forty mules with packs if everyone's on horseback," answered Big Bob.

"Yeah, I've only got twenty pack trees, but I've got twenty extra-large saddle bags. If you put two sets of saddle bags on each mule they'll hold as much as packs."

"Okay, do you have plenty of rope?"

"Sure, Big Bob—even extra—got to keep it on hand for lead ropes and such."

Big Bob took the last drag from his cigarette and stomped it out. "Where do you want the wagon and horses?"

"Just bring them over by the barn's tack room. Unload the saddles and put your horses in the corral with the big water trough," answered Dan.

"Okay, but I've just had a thought, will we need extra canteens?"

"No, you shore won't. Every other rock up there has pure spring water running out from under it. Best tasting water you'll ever drink," answered Dan.

"Well, Dan, you might as well come on over to the chuck wagon for breakfast. Mary's an ex-boardinghouse cook, and she'll be using up her extra flour on this morning's biscuits and gravy."

"Sounds good, Big Bob, but I've got to get those packs rounded up and my wife Betty already got some bacon and eggs ready for me by now, so I'll check with you later," grinned Dan.

"All right," Big Bob said as he mounted Stumpy and headed back to the chuck wagon where Mary had breakfast in full swing. The men were sitting around eating. Big Bob went to the tailgate where the food is and helped himself to some biscuits and gravy. Mary was busy sorting pots and pans into packs.

"Well, did Dan have enough mules for this expedition?" asked Mac.

"Shore did," answered Big Bob. "Even more than what we needed. I dealt for forty mules."

"Forty mules!" exclaimed Lee Roy. "Isn't that more than we need?"

"Not by the time we put the supplies on the mules. With the picks, shovels, pans for panning, cooking utensils, hardtack, and other groceries we'll have all of them loaded," answered Big Bob.

"How much did the mules cost us?" asked Mac.

"The extra horses and extra saddles plus the chuck wagon," replied Big Bob.

"Sounds like a pretty fair trade to me," said Lee Roy.

"Yeah, soon as we get done eating we'll move the extra horses into Dan's corral with the big water trough. We'll need to park the chuck wagon next to the tack room," said Big Bob.

"I'm shore gonna miss this chuck wagon," said Mary.

"I'm sure you will, Mary. I'll tell you what, Mac will oversee the loading of your groceries and packs, and Cruz and Pancho will load the mining supplies," grinned Big Bob. "Emanuel, you and Lee Roy will be the rope men. Y'all ready?" Everyone nodded. "Okay, then let's get started."

About two hours later all the mules were loaded, lead ropes to horses were tied, and Mac the old mountain man took the lead, with Big Bob and Mary right behind.

"Well, folks we're only fifty miles from the area that Pancho's ring was supposed to come from."

"All right, Mac, there will be no doubting Thomases among us. Even if there's no gold, the hunting and fishing up this way is terrific," stated Lee Roy.

"Yeah, I can think of other places to hunt where the Indians aren't so savage," replied Mac.

"Well if the Indians get the drop on y'all, just call for Mary," teased Cruz.

"That's right," answered Mary. "Me and this ole greener will give a good account of ourselves!"

"Just ask them outlaws down at the Red River," smiled Big Bob. The laughter was joined in by one and all.

The pack mules that Dan had traded and sold them had been

trail-broken for years. They had little or no trouble with these mules and made excellent time from Broken Bow to Mountain Fork River.

The terrain began to change from gentle hills to steep sloping mountains. The woods were so quiet that they could hear the river rushing over rocks a mile before they got there. When they arrived, all the horses and mules drank from the stream. The men refilled their canteens, and Mary fetched water for a pot of coffee.

Mac was happy as a lark smelling the rich pine trees, and the seemingly fresher air in the mountains had a good effect on him.

"Mary, if I was to catch a mess of fish would you cook them?" asked Mac.

"Shore would," smiled Mary.

"Maybe I'd better help, Mac," commented Lee Roy as he found some line and hooks.

"Would *Señor* Lee Roy mind if Popcorn and I join this fishing expedition?" asked Cruz as he carried his rooster down the riverbank with him.

"Naw, come right along. Just don't let that ornery rooster eat the bait," laughed Lee Roy.

The place where they had stopped was a rapids, then the river dropped off into a large pool before it went further south. The rapids made a natural feeding place for channel cats. In less than thirty minutes, the fishermen had over ten catfish apiece. They were having a good time and hated to stop, but being true woodsmen, they never caught nor killed more than what was necessary for their survival.

Mary was pleased when they brought the fish to her. She quickly filleted the fish and fed the scraps to Popcorn and his hens. After supper the men drew straws to see who would keep the first watch. Emanuel got the first watch and Pancho got the last.

The men took their bedrolls off their horses and laid them down on a sandy portion of the river bank.

NINE

The smell of bacon frying and biscuits baking in the Dutch oven brought the cowboys-turned-prospectors to life. They needed no one to wake them; life on the trail was hard and meals were few and far between. Fortunately they had Mary for a cook. These past few weeks seemed like a vacation to them. Mac had gotten up early and helped Mary, then he had a cup of coffee and wandered off down by the river to give thought to the day's journey and what route to take.

"Morning, Mary."

"Morning, Big Bob."

"I shore do like these pine trees."

"Yeah, me too. Someday I'll cut us some logs and build us a cabin."

"Really, Big Bob?"

"Sure will. I tell you what, when we get to the headwaters of the Kiamichi River we might just build a small cabin with a corral as a base for our operations."

"Say, that's a good idea," thought Lee Roy out loud. Mac came walking up and put his two cents worth in.

"Won't take too long to build, plus we can have a rock and mud fireplace."

"Nothing fancy, but it'll keep the snow and rain out this winter," mused Big Bob. "Besides, we'll need a place to rest and store our supplies."

"Well, I'll keep an eye out for a good location," threw in Mac. "It's something to think about while we're riding today."

Cruz and Pancho were already rolling up their bedrolls when Mac gave the quiet sign with his right hand. Then he pointed to a knoll across the river. There stood a beautiful eight-point buck. Everybody grinned as he spotted them and bounded off into the woods.

No one had even attempted to shoot him, because they would have to clean him and pack the meat all day before they could cook it. Why try to store something when it was probably in reasonable supply down the trail?

Mac was first in the saddle and led them through several twists and turns as he discovered game trails alongside the river. They traveled from sunup to sundown, passing through God's most beautiful country, the Kiamichi Mountains. When they camped for the night, they were tired and weary.

"We made good time today, but I'm wore out," complained Mac.

"Yeah, me too," answered Big Bob.

Cruz and Pancho came over to where Mac and Big Bob were talking.

"*Señor* Mac, this bend in the river is very large and turns due east."

"Yes, Pancho, I believe this is the big bend that your Indian friend was telling us about. From here it is only ten miles to where this river turns north."

"*Sí Señor* Mac, then he said, 'Go north till you reach the Kiamichi River.'"

"Okay. That's about eight miles from Mountain Fork. By tomorrow night we should be very close to the gold," said Mac.

"Hooray!" shouted Lee Roy, joined by Cruz, Emanuel, Pancho, Samuel, Big Bob, and Mary.

"The sooner I get my share of gold, the sooner I'll have a gamecock ranch. Ole Popcorn will be stud of a whole bunch of hens!" said Cruz.

"Yeah, the sooner I'll have my horse ranch," chimed Pancho.

"You can bet I'll have my old .50 caliber Hawken gold plated," the heads turned as Mary spoke. "I think I'll have a fancy restaurant."

"And I will have enough money to eat at yore restaurant. Speaking of eating, what's for supper?" asked Big Bob.

"Looks like we're having beef jerky. In the morning after a good night's sleep, I'll make a big meal. Right now, I'm give out," said Mary.

"Shore, Mary, we understand." Big Bob was hungry as a bear, but also very tired. It was his and Cruz's turn to nightwatch.

The rest of them got their bedrolls off of their horses or mules. Even Mac, the old mountain man, was relieved to camp for the night. After hobbling the mules, the sound of the river and men chewing beef jerky was all that could be heard.

The night passed uneventfully and the next morning everyone woke refreshed and hungry. After the big meal that Mary promised, everyone was eager to travel the last leg of their journey. When they came to the bend in Mountain Fork, Mac led off due north to Kiamichi River.

The mountains were not as steep as they had been earlier. However, travel was still difficult. The ride alongside Mountain Fork was easier that the terrain they now traveled through. Soft pine needles quieted the sound of the mules and horses.

As they neared the Kiamichi, rocks became huge boulders. Walls and rock cliffs were everywhere; Mac spied a knoll with large pine trees.

"Hey, Big Bob?"

"Yeah Mac," answered Big Bob.

"You see that knoll over yonder with the pine trees and easy access to the water?" pointed out Mac.

"Uh-huh."

Mary rode up beside them. "Oh, that's a beautiful place, Big Bob. Let's camp there tonight to see if we like it."

"Good idea," replied Big Bob.

After they found the way to the knoll, the sun was all but gone from the sky.

"Looks like another beef jerky supper tonight," Mary informed the men.

The men knew that tomorrow would be a good day to eat, as camp would be permanently set up along with a kitchen. Anyway, they were all glad to finally be there.

"Ya know, Big Bob, we've been real lucky not getting snake bit," stated Mac.

"Yeah, Mac, that's true, but we've got rocks and pits plenty of water so we're gonna have snakes," replied Big Bob.

"True enough. Perhaps we shouldn't tempt them. What say we take our bedrolls, tie ropes to these pine trees, and use them like hammocks?" suggested Mac.

"That's good thinking, Mac," answered Big Bob.

Big Bob explained Mac's theory to the rest of the little band. Everyone but Emanuel liked it.

"*Sí, Señor* Big Bob, I've slept on the ground most all of my life, and I'm skeered of sleeping so high above the ground. What if one of the ropes should break? Poor ole Emanuel would be banged to the ground."

"Well if that's the way you feel, go ahead and sleep on the ground. Don't blame me if you get snake bit," said Big Bob, shaking his head.

It was Mac's and Lee Roy's turn to keep watch. Lee Roy had first watch. It was quiet all night, with only a few hoot owls making any noise at all. The mighty Kiamichi River wasn't much more than a creek up here close to its headwater. It sounded like a babbling brook.

The smell of coffee, bacon, biscuits, and gravy was more than enough to bring the tough prospectors to life. Mac was wanting a cup of coffee. Lee Roy wanted some food and was getting a cup of coffee when Cruz came up, all excited.

"*Señor* Lee Roy, Emanuel has a six-foot rattlesnake coiled on his belly."

"Oh, hell." Lee Roy laid his food and coffee down and headed for Emanuel's sleeping bag.

There were Samuel and Pancho, standing helpless as the big rattler held its head up in the striking position and gave its rattles a warning shake. Obviously, the snake had crawled onto Emanuel's belly during the night to stay warm.

"What we gonna do?" asked Pancho as Emanuel held perfectly still.

" How about we shoot it in the head?" suggested Cruz.

"Lee Roy's the best shot," commented Mac.

"Yeah, but I'm gonna need the big Hawken. It'll blow the sucker's head plumb off," Lee Roy said as he headed for his old black powder rifle.

"I'm glad I put a fresh load in this thang last night while I was on guard duty. Emanuel, if you agree with me shooting that rattler, blink your eyes once," commanded Lee Roy. Emanuel slowly blinked his eyes once.

Lee Roy steadied his old rifle on a rock as he watched the snake through his sights. Exhaling slowly, he squeezed the trigger. The sound of the explosion was deafening, the snake flew through the air for about two feet, but before it could hit the ground, Emanuel rolled away from it and was on his feet in a flash. The snake writhed and twisted, but it was dead.

"Thank you, *Señor* Lee Roy," said Emanuel.

"You're welcome," replied Lee Roy.

"Let's skin this rascal and have fried rattlesnake for lunch. He was gonna bite me, but I'm gonna bite him," laughed Emanuel.

"Gonna sleep on the ground again tonight?" asked Mac.

"No sir, *Señor* Mac," answered Emanuel.

"Good."

"Let's go eat breakfast before it gets cold," said Big Bob.

Later that day, Big Bob and Lee Roy were looking at some of the large pine trees on top of the knoll.

"If we were to fell these big ones and notch them, they would make a good foundation for our house," said Big Bob.

"Yeah, we could pull the smaller ones with mules to build the walls," added Lee Roy.

"OK, perhaps a sod roof and rock fireplace," added Big Bob.

"Right, we could use one side of the cabin for part of the corral," stated Lee Roy.

"OK, let's get started," said Big Bob as he got his ax and ran into Mary.

"We're beginning to build the cabin. We've already spotted some fine timber," Big Bob told her.

"Oh, Big Bob, a cabin in the woods."

"Yes, Mary, and it'll have a fireplace, too."

"That will make the work easier for me. Cooking has been quite a chore for me out in the open," Mary told him.

"Well, in about three days you'll have a fireplace and a split log table with benches," grinned Big Bob.

"Yes, that will be handy," smiled Mary.

In the days that followed, the men set an easy pace, for the pine wood was easy to work with. The logs fit together snugly and needed little chinking. However, selecting rocks and building a fireplace was a little more difficult.

Finding rocks flat on one or both sides consumed time. Emanuel would walk his mules along behind him and collect rocks and place them in the large saddle bags. Then he would take them to Cruz and Pancho, who were building the fireplace.

"This is more like art than masonry," said Emanuel.

"*Sí amigo*, placing this rock and locking it with this rock is like building a house of cards," replied Cruz.

"*Sí amigo*, but the soot from the fire will help lock them in place," said Pancho.

"Big Bob has built a nice table that will comfortably seat us all," states Pancho.

"Yes, but those rawhide hinges on the door will only last a few months," said Cruz.

"*Si*, but by then we will be rich!" said Emanuel.

"I hope so," said Pancho.

Mary looked the cabin over as she began to move her pots and pans in. "Big Bob, that's a right nice table you've built us."

"Thanks."

"Just think, tomorrow we'll all be able to go and hunt for gold," mused Mary.

"Yes, the cabin's finished, and we're ready for cold weather," stated Big Bob.

TEN

The next morning everyone was up early, anticipating the search for gold. Mary's breakfast was unusually large with fried potatoes, gravy, biscuits, and salt pork. The coffee was extra good.

"Mary this coffee is shore good."

"Yes, Mary, it shore is," assured Mac.

"And I know what makes it taste so good," teased Lee Roy.

"What is the secret?" asked Mary.

"Well, I'll tell ya. It's the water," drawled Lee Roy.

"The water," Mary said in surprise to his answer.

"Shore enough. That pool of water you're fetching out of is as pure as it gets. That's the headwaters of the Kiamichi. Only a few know that there is a large spring which starts it; from there it is fed by tributaries and flows into the Red River."

"Well, thank you, Lee Roy, for explaining why the coffee tastes so good," teased Mary.

"Yeah, Mr. Schoolmaster, only question I have is where is the gold?" asked Big Bob.

"Well now, let's see, the way the old Indian told us was to take Mountain Fork River north from Broken Bow till it turned east, then when the river went north to keep going till we found the Kiamichi River head upstream till we found the gold," answered Lee Roy.

"Well, by my reckoning, we're right on track," mused Mac.

"Okay, Pancho, you stay with Mary while the rest of us go in teams of two to explore," Big Bob said, starting to make plans.

"*Señor* Big Bob, my gold ring is very, very heavy and my hand eagerly awaits the burden of more gold," said Pancho.

"Okay, Pancho, maybe Emanuel is not so eager?" asked Big Bob as his eyes fell on Emanuel.

"*Sí, Señor* Big Bob, Emanuel is not so eager as Pancho," Emanuel answered.

Everybody laughed because Emanuel answered so slowly that his intentions were clearly understood: a day in camp with an early siesta.

Samuel and Pancho decided to ride mules as they panned for gold. Mac and Lee Roy decided to pan likely looking areas on foot. Big Bob and Cruz thought they'd ride to the spring and back for an informal survey of the river and what formations to inspect at a later date. They also carried pans for gold.

Mac and Lee Roy had walked about three hundred yards upstream when they found what they were looking for and settled down to do some panning.

"That's some pretty rich-looking rock on the other side of this pool," said Lee Roy.

"Aw, t'aint bad, but the wash pan will tell the tale if there's any gold in these rocks," stated Mac.

"Shore is clear."

"Let's muddy it up a mite."

Samuel and Pancho had ridden with Big Bob and Cruz until Cruz spotted a bend in the river which made it flow like a creek over a table of rock, then into a large pool.

"If there was ever a nugget of gold in Indian Territory, it ought to be in that sand," said Pancho as he dismounted his mule and grabbed his gold pan.

"Wait for me!" cried Samuel as he grabbed his pan.

Big Bob looked at Cruz and shook his head as he said, "They've got fever."

"*Sí Señor* Big Bob, gold fever."

"Let's see what's on the other side of this bend," stated Big Bob.

Cruz nodded his head in agreement as he turned his horse's head upstream. Rounding the bend, they found the river's headwaters. Gushing out of the side of the mountain rock was a seven-foot-wide stream of clear water, tumbling down onto the river bed and splashing off some rocks into little pools. At one such pool a turkey gobbler was getting a drink. Across from him a large buck deer was also drinking. When Big Bob saw the buck, he drew his .45 Colt and nailed him straight through the heart.

"Nice shot, *Señor* Big Bob," congratulated Cruz. "We shall have fresh venison for many days!"

"Shore beats going hungry, but I almost had a case of buck fever," said Big Bob.

"Why is that?"

"Because the sight of him drinking at the spring seemed almost sacred," answered Big Bob.

"*Sí señor*, I was struck by the beauty of the mountain spring also."

"Time we clean him and start back it will be nightfall."

"*Sí señor*." Meanwhile the first team of Mac and Lee Roy was getting pretty disgusted.

"I ain't never seen such a natural pretty place as this provide me with so much work and no reward," bitched Lee Roy.

"I hear ya, old buddy, but this ain't like punching cows," said Mac.

"How's that?"

"Well, when you're punching cows and you're successful, you get paid a limited amount. That amount will give you a toehold on your monthly bills. However, if you find this here gold, you'll have a foothold and be able to stand head and shoulders above yore financial obligations. Such amount of freedom doesn't come easily and requires a determined mind," stated Mac.

"Well, hush my mouth. I didn't know the old mountain man understood money."

"I don't or I wouldn't be here."

"Where would you be?"

"Hell, if I had money I'd be running the finest well-dressed string of whores New Orleans ever seen."

"Yeah, and I'd be yore best customer."

"I doubt that."

"Why?"

"No credit!" laughed Mac.

"You old goat," laughed Lee Roy.

"Shoot, we may as well head back to camp," said Mac.

"Yeah, all this work's making me hungry," said Lee Roy.

The second team of Samuel and Pancho had fared no better than the first.

"You know, Pancho, I bet Mary has that deer meat cooking slow and easy."

"*Sí señor*, I'll bet Big Bob and Cruz are eating a mouthful right now."

"*Sí*, when they rode by, *Señor* Cruz was pointing at the deer and rubbing his hand on his belly.

"*Sí*, always joking, that one."

"*Sí*, this area here is a joke also."

"*Sí señor*, let's go fer supper."

Big Bob, Cruz, Mary, Emanuel, Mac, and Lee Roy were waiting at camp, expecting to hear good news from Samuel and Pancho's findings. One look, however, at their faces, and everyone at camp knew they had found nothing.

"How's the deer steaks?"

"They're great, Pancho!" Big Bob smiled as he asked, "Is your other hand heavy with gold?"

"No sir, Big Bob, it is not, but tomorrow it will be."

"Yeah, I shore hope so," remarked Lee Roy.

While Pancho and Samuel put their mules in the corral with the others, Mary prepared them two plates brimming over with deer steaks.

"I noticed some clouds to the north of us about sundown," said Mac.

"We might be in fer a little rain," said Lee Roy.

"Little—hell—when it rains in the mountains, it pours through the pine trees like a lake turned upside down!" explained Big Bob.

"Well, I'm glad we have a sod roof over split logs," Mary said as she gathered in her day's washing.

"You know, Mary's never been through a thunderstorm in the mountains," smiled Big Bob.

"And what's so different about a thunderstorm in the mountains from anyplace else?" asked Mary.

"Well, fer one thang the lighting and thunder are very close," explained Mac. "You might want to stick something in your ears."

"What's best?" asked Mary.

"Cotton's best," answered Mac.

"I know what's better than cotton," stated Big Bob.

"What's that?"

"No storm," answered Big Bob.

While Pancho ate his deer steak, Samuel cut himself another big steak also. Cruz was sitting down at the table thinking aloud.

"*Señor* Big Bob, if that old Indian was accurate in his directions, we may be a little too far east," mused Cruz.

"That's entirely possible. What say we do our panning further downstream tomorrow?"

"Suits me to a tee," stated Mac.

"Well, Emanuel is the best cook's helper out of this whole bunch and has the least amount of gold fever," interrupted Mary.

"All right, then unless someone sprains an ankle or something, we'll leave Emanuel on permanent camp duty, if that's OK with everyone?" asked Big Bob.

Everyone nodded their heads in agreement.

"All right, let's leave the two-man teams as is," suggested Big Bob.

Mary had finished stacking the supper dishes when she asked, "Big Bob, would you show me the Big Dipper?"

"Why shore, come, let's go fer a walk."

Outside the cabin, Big Bob asked, "What's the matter, honey?"

"Oh Big Bob, what if all this is just one big goose chase?"

"Well, I'll tell ya what, we're up here in the Kiamichi Mountains amongst the finest hunting and fishing God ever created. We'll enjoy this trip as long as it's enjoyed. When the fun stops, we'll head back to civilization."

"One thing's fer sure, we ain't spending any money out here in these woods," said Mary.

"That's right, and when we go back we'll eat and drink at the finest restaurants and stay at the finest hotels till we decide what we want to do next," said Big Bob.

"Well, while you're deciding what to do next we ought to buy a small ranch fer the youngins to be raised on," said Mary.

"What youngins?"

"The one we're gonna have!"

"Oh, Mary, I'm so, so happy. How far along are you?" asked Big Bob.

"Any where from six weeks to two months."

"Should we trip out?"

"Naw, give it a couple of months, some gold might come in handy raising a youngin."

"That is, if there's any gold," stated Big Bob.

"Do you doubt it?" asked Mary.

"After today I began to wonder."

"Well, I've wondered this whole trip," stated Mary.

"Then why did you come along?" asked Big Bob.

"Because of you."

"Me!"

"That's right, I'm in love with you," sighed Mary.

"I love you too, honey." Big Bob smiled.

The stars were shining bright that night in Indian Territory, and the clouds from the north never did reach far enough south to block the view of the stars for the young lovers.

ELEVEN

The next morning was foggy; there was little wind as the cowboys-turned-prospectors had their breakfast.

"Deer meat and biscuits, I shore do like mountain breakfasts," stated Mac with a smile.

"Especially if you ain't doing the cooking," laughed Lee Roy.

"Well I'm full as a tick and ready to find my fortune in gold," announced Big Bob as he raised up from the table. Walking across the room, he picked up his hat and placed it on his head. Stepping outside, he checked his pistol to be sure it was fully loaded. One never knew when a wild hog or feisty panther would cross his path. The rest of the men came outside the cabin, placing fresh chews of tobacco in their mouths, getting ready for the day's activity.

"Good hunting," said Big Bob as he slapped Samuel and Pancho on their backs. "Y'all get the first pool west of where Mary's been getting the cooking water."

"*Sí Señor* Big Bob," agreed Pancho.

Mac, Lee Roy, Big Bob, and Cruz rode further down the Kiamichi, coming to a bend about a quarter-mile further than where Samuel and Pancho were.

"That sand's a likely looking place," commented Mac as he spit a stream of brownish fluid from his mouth.

"Yeah, let's start about the middle of the bend," suggested Lee Roy.

"Well, y'all look like you've got it figured out," Big Bob said as he and Cruz passed on by, going further down the river.

Big Bob and Cruz rode about two hundred yards when the rocks and boulders became impassable for their mules. Leading their mules, they followed the river as close as they could.

"Damn these rocks," bitched Big Bob.

"*Sí señor*, a pool and a bend that arches past these rocks," commented Cruz. "Should we go further or pan for gold in this pool?"

"Well I can't pass this pool," replied Big Bob.

"*Sí señor*, I'll explore the area and be back in an hour or so to help."

"Shore, go ahead," Big Bob replied as he got his pan out.

Cruz left his mule with Big Bob's as he headed on downriver. Exploring the giant boulders around the pool, he slowly worked his way downstream. Finding a chimney, he crawled down into the rocks. Being careful to check that there were no smooth places worn by snakes, he proceeded into a natural tunnel. Seeing light and hearing water, he continued until he came out behind and under the waterfall.

"Big Bob!" Cruz hollered.

"What the heck!" exclaimed Big Bob as he turned loose his gold pan and fell back on the sand, drawing his revolver.

"Don't shoot, *Señor* Big Bob," shouted Cruz as he emerged through the waterfalls.

"Well, I'll be damned!" exclaimed Big Bob. "How in the world did you get back there?"

"I found a chimney that led into a short tunnel that ended behind this waterfall," answered Cruz.

"Talk about a natural secret passage. Take me and show me," said Big Bob.

"Shore, follow me."

Cruz led Big Bob back into the waterfalls and into the tunnel.

"Man, this is something," stated Big Bob.

Coming to the end of the tunnel they climbed out through the chimney.

"This place is a natural escape. With the hidden hole between these boulders a man could lose his pursuers in a hurry," commented Big Bob.

"*Sí señor*," Cruz agreed as he crawled higher on the giant rock next to the chimney. "This would be a good lookout post."

"Shore would," agreed Big Bob. "What can you see?"

"I see the bend around those huge ancient rocks. That leads into some strange looking formation," Cruz told him.

"What do you mean strange?" questioned Big Bob.

"Well, Big Bob, it's off to the right of the river rising out of the ground."

"Let's go have a closer look," mused Big Bob.

Crossing the boulders and following the river, they found the formation, which looked like a giant *L* with a leg on bottom. They walked around looking, feeling, smelling of this rocky, natural creation. Big Bob picked up a few pieces of broken rocks for samples.

"Looks like a geological nightmare," commented Big Bob.

"*Sí señor*, this whole area is carved by God's hand."

"Yes, Cruz, so pretty but unusual, with ordinary things transformed into a unique pattern."

"*Sí señor*, perhaps this is a holy place."

"Could be," agreed Big Bob.

"Let's go back to the waterfalls, perhaps there may be

some nuggets for us," suggested Big Bob.

Heading back, Big Bob and Cruz heard a loud noise like a boulder being pushed off a cliff. Moving forward with caution, they slowly rounded a hillside where a large buck ran flat out for the other side of the hill. As the buck disappeared into the brush, a feline hunter trailed him, bounding from one rock to another as she crossed the water.

"That's a pretty large mountain lion," commented Big Bob as Cruz raised his eyebrows and nodded his head in agreement.

"I hope she didn't spook the mules into running off," Big Bob thought aloud.

Hurriedly, they headed toward the waterfall where they found the mules flaring their noses and nervously pacing about.

"They smell the cat," said Big Bob.

"*Sí señor*, but they'll calm down now that we're here," assured Cruz.

"Oh, I hope so, this place has an eerie feel to it."

"*Sí Señor* Big Bob, but perhaps it wouldn't be so eerie if we found some gold."

"Perhaps," replied Big Bob as he headed for the gold pan he'd discarded earlier.

While the team of Big Bob and Cruz had been exploring, the team of Mac and Lee Roy had been panning in earnest.

"We've been panning all day, and there's not even one itty-bitty grain of gold in our pans," griped Lee Roy.

"Yeah, I know what you're talking about," agreed Mac. "I've been in the mountains before where we'd find very little gold. But we did find some."

"I wished we'd find some, 'cause I'm getting tired of all this panning for nothing."

"We're just not in the right spot today," explained Mac as he carried his pan over to his pack sack and loaded it. "No more fer me today."

"Nor me either," replied Lee Roy as he sat down on the river bank, pulled the makings out of his shirt pocket, and began to roll himself a smoke.

"We've been upstream, downstream, and panned every grain of sand in two pools without so much as a shiny rock," Lee Roy said as he lit his smoke.

"Well, we've got two other teams working east and west of us, maybe they'll find something," stated Mac as he tore another bite off his plug of tobacco.

Pancho and Samuel had not fared any better, their gold pans were broke-in, their backs were broke, and Pancho was cussing the Indian who had sold him the ring and told him about the gold. Samuel's short temper had gotten the best of him, and he flung his gold hunting pan downstream and stomped off toward the bank, where he rolled himself a smoke.

"I think it's time we called it quits fer today," Pancho said as he kindly walked over to pick up Samuel's pan.

"*Sí señor*," agreed Samuel.

"What's this?" asked Pancho as he poured the sand out of Samuel's pan. Something shiny fell onto the bank along with the river sand.

"Probably an old shirt button," Samuel said sarcastically.

"Well, I be damned!" smiled Pancho as he threw it up in the air and caught it with his hand.

"What is it?" asked Samuel disheartedly.

"A solid gold nugget!"

"What? Lemme see," slurred Samuel with excitement.

"Shore, catch!" With that, Pancho threw the nugget to Samuel.

"Whoa, it shore is," said Samuel as he caught it in his hand. Examining it closer, he said, "This one's about the size of your ring."

"Now I'll have two rings," said Pancho.

"Oh, no, it came out of my pan," protested Samuel.

"*Sí señor*, but I'm the one who picked the pan up," grinned Pancho.

About then, Big Bob and the others came out of the brush and upon the sand.

"What are y'all arguing about?" asked Big Bob.

"This!" said Samuel as he threw the nugget to Big Bob.

"Oh boy, lookee here!" Big Bob said, very excited, as he threw the nugget to Lee Roy.

"I take back everything I've said today." Lee Roy smiled as he handed it to Mac.

"Whooee! A sure 'nough gold nugget," yelled Mac.

"Let me see it," commanded Cruz.

"Shore," said Mac as he handed it to Cruz.

"Well, men, we're very close to being rich. Let's not lose our heads. It's getting late and the gold will be here tomorrow. Why don't we head for camp?" suggested Big Bob.

In there hearts they wanted to stay and look some more, but their minds knew it would soon be dark. Rather than look in the dark, they'd just as soon help themselves to Mary's good cooking. After they'd made it to the little log cabin, everyone sat around trying to eat supper.

"What's wrong with y'all?" asked Mary.

"Better ask Pancho," smiled Big Bob.

"Pancho, what is it?" Mary inquired.

"Enough gold to make me another ring!" Pancho said as he laid the nugget on the split log table.

"Oh yes," cried Mary as she picked it up off the table and held it up to the kerosene lamp for a closer look.

"This means it wasn't a wild-goose chase after all!" quipped Big Bob.

"Now, Big Bob, I wasn't the only one who thought this might be a wild-goose chase," said Mary.

"Yeah, I know each and every one of us had our doubts," Big Bob said as he looked his friends in their eyes.

"Well, just because Pancho found a nugget doesn't mean we'll get rich. But at least we know there is gold in them there hills," laughed Mac.

"Right now I could use a drink," smiled Lee Roy.

"Just happen to have one, pardner," Mac said as he walked to the corner of the log cabin and retrieved a bottle of whiskey from his old saddle bags. After he took a drink, he handed the bottle to Lee Roy.

"No doubt about it," crowed Lee Roy. "This here's good corn whiskey." He passed the bottle back to Mac who in turn handed it to Big Bob.

"Glug...glug. Nothing like a little drink to end the day," Big Bob said as he passed the bottle to Mary.

"Thank ya, Big Bob."

"Yore welcome, Mary."

With that last salutation, Mary took a medium-sized drink and passed the bottle to Pancho. "To the man of the hour."

"*Sí señora*," Pancho said as he accepted the bottle. Taking a large drink, he offered what was left to Samuel. "Here's to your short temper."

"*Sí señor*," Samuel said, accepting the bottle. "Here is to good luck and good fortune." Then he drank half of what was left, passing the bottle to Emanuel while he was still swallowing.

Emanuel took the bottle and said, "Here's to a good night's sleep." Polishing the last of the whiskey off, he took the bottle outside.

"Well, I agree with Emanuel," yawned Big Bob. "A good night's rest and we might be able to find some more gold tomorrow."

"Yeah, yore right. Good night," said Mac.

TWELVE

The night passed uneventfully. It was Mac's late night on guard. He was first to have a cup of coffee. Big Bob had just dressed and walked to the table.

"Morning, Mac."

"Morning, Big Bob. I've been thinking that this pool in front of our cabin might have some gold in it also."

"I bet it does, Mac. However, I'm sure everyone will want to work the discovery hole first."

"Yeah, me too, but later I'd like to work this pool out front."

"Say, Mac, just before the discovery yesterday, Cruz and I found some formation sticking out of the ground." Reaching into his pocket, Big Bob produced the rock he had taken earlier for samples.

"Well, Big Bob, these samples indicate a shale formation. Sometimes they get turned on end. Often coal is found close to shale formations. Some geologists believe that's what coal was before it was coal."

"You reckon there's coal around here?" asked Big Bob.

"Yeah, I bet there is," said Mac.

"What's all this about coal?" asked Cruz as he sat down to have his morning coffee.

"Uh, Mac says that formation we stumbled across yesterday was shale," replied Big Bob.

"Oh, yes I see." Cruz understood.

About this time, everyone seemed to be up and dressed. Mary had biscuits and deer meat ready. They could hardly eat fast enough, like children at Christmas who can't wait to open their Christmas presents.

When the men got done with their breakfast, they got their gold pans and headed for the discovery hole.

"Hey, *Señor* Big Bob," said Cruz.

"Yes."

"Bet I get a nugget 'fore you do," teased Cruz.

"Oh, give me a break!" said Big Bob as he headed for the sand by the water's edge.

Pancho winked at Samuel. They'd panned there the day before. Heading for the spot where Samuel had flung his pan, Pancho and Samuel began panning in earnest. Mac, Cruz, and Lee Roy began panning in the area close to Samuel.

Everyone was hard at work, not making a sound. They toiled endlessly as the day wore on. When afternoon came they sat on the bank, smoking and eating a snack.

"I just don't understand it," griped Big Bob. "We can't find a single grain of gold here."

"Yet yesterday," Lee Roy picked up where Big Bob left off, "there was a nugget big enough to choke a horse."

"*Sí señor*, it doesn't make any sense to me either," Pancho said.

"Well, maybe there isn't any gold here. Maybe it's upstream," Mac informed them between chews.

"The pool in front of the cabin—wouldn't that be something," laughed Big Bob.

"Stranger things have happened," said a wild-eyed Mac.

"Perhaps the mother lode is located at the cabin's pool. What say we go up there for the rest of the day?" asked Big Bob.

"I'd say that was a good ideal," replied Lee Roy.

"*Sí señor*," Pancho and Samuel said in unison.

So the weary gold hunters walked a few hundred yards up to the cabin pool. Mary came out to greet them by the pool.

"Are we rich yet?" she asked.

"No not yet, hon."

"What are y'all doing to my water hole?" she asks.

"Well, the gold experts have decided that this is the only pool we haven't panned. There's a good chance that this may be the spot!" explained Big Bob.

"I hope so 'cause I'm a'gonna have to get my cooking water further upstream after y'all muddy this hole up with yore panning," complained Mary.

"Honey, it will be a small price to pay if we're successful," smiled Big Bob.

While Big Bob and Mary were fussing, the others were wasting no daylight as they began panning.

"One thang about panning this close to the cabin, we can tell when supper is ready," Lee Roy said as he flared his nostrils, sniffing the air like a bear.

"Gold may be in short supply, but the humor is plentiful," Mac said. "Back to panning, slave."

"Yes suh!" laughed Lee Roy.

They panned till Mary came out of the cabin and banged on a frying pan. "Chow's on."

"Well, at least we know when quitting time is around here," said Cruz.

As they were eating, Mary told Big Bob, "The last of the deer meat will be for breakfast in the morning."

"All right, I'll send Mac or Lee Roy hunting—whichever wants to go."

"I'll be happy to hunt for meat, as the panning is pretty boring," said Lee Roy.

"Thanks," said Mary.

"Tell me something, Mac?"

"Yeah, Big Bob."

"If the gold we're finding is in large nuggets, then why aren't we finding any small ones?" asked Big Bob.

"I haven't thought about that, but maybe alongside of the discovery hole there is a vein," answered Mac.

"OK, let's look for one in the morning," said Big Bob.

Everyone went to bed early that night, no drinking or joking; everyone was pretty discouraged. About midnight a storm blew in. Heavy rain awoke Mary.

"Big Bob, it's a storm."

"Yes, Mary, it is, sounds like a bad one too."

The lighting flashed through the cracks in the cabin.

Big Bob counted, "One...two..." Boom! The thunder cracked. All the men sat up in their bedrolls.

"Uh-oh, that one was close!" said someone in the dark.

Flash! "One..." Boom! "That one's even closer," said Lee Roy.

"Yeah, but it was east of here." Flash! "One...two..." Boom! "See there, that thundercloud has passed us by," explained Big Bob.

Flash! "One...two...three..." Boom! "Oh, Big Bob, that cloud's gone for good," said Mary, hoping.

"No honey, that one's coming this way."

Flash. "One...two..." Boom! Flash. "One...two..." Boom! Flash. "One...two..." Boom! Flash. "One..." Boom! Flash. "One..." Boom! Flash. Boom! Crack! Crash!

"What's happening?" Mary asked.

"Sounds like lightning hit a tree close."

Flash "One..." Boom! The thunder drowned out further conversation, besides everyone was deaf. Flash. "One..." Boom!

"I hope the mules don't run off," Emanuel prayed out loud.

Flash. "One...two..." Boom! The rain began again, coming

down harder and harder, sheet after sheet pelting their hastily built cabin. Water was leaking in everywhere. Someone lit one of the kerosene lamps. Flash! "One...two...three..." Boom! Kaboom!

"I hope the lightning's past us," spoke Lee Roy.

"I think it is," answered Mac.

"Oh, this place is a mess," Mary cried.

"Don't worry, honey," Big Bob said as he slid his arm around Mary's shoulders. "We'll help you clean up tomorrow."

"Oh, thanks, Big Bob."

The others had packed mud from the dirt floor into the bottom cracks of the cabin, stopping the flash flood of water. They gathered around the split log table and smoked a few cigarettes as the storm's fury pushed further south. Rearranging their beds and shaking the water off, they went back to bed.

"Mary, are you ready?" asked Big Bob.

"Yes, honey," Mary said as Big Bob turned out the light.

The next morning there was no firewood dry enough to burn. Mac and Lee Roy went to check on the mules and found a large pine tree had fallen across the makeshift gate and smashed it to the ground. Needless to say, the mules were scattered across the mountains. Cruz and Pancho went to get water for coffee and found the river was swollen to twice its normal size.

"Pretty rough storm," commented Big Bob.

"Yeah, it'll be tomorrow before we get back to prospecting," said Mac.

"Let's get some kindling and dry some firewood out. Maybe that will lift everyone's spirits," commented Big Bob.

After they finally got a small fire going, they added some small dead pine tree limbs until they dried and ignited into a good fire. Soon as they had a bed of coals, Mary made a pot of coffee.

"Looks like quite a bit of damage to the old sod roof," commented Mac as he drank his coffee.

"Yeah, we'll have to fix the roof and round up the mules before dark," Big Bob replied.

"Well, the water's too high to prospect anyway," reported Cruz.

"I think by the time we fix the roof and rebuild the gate it'll be mid-afternoon. Perhaps by then the horses and mules will be hungry enough for some corn after grazing on this mountain bluestem," Big Bob said, thinking out loud.

"You know for a flatlander of a cowhand, you have some pretty good ideas sometimes," smiled Mac as he finished his coffee.

"I've got a good idea," piped up Mary.

"What's that?" asked Big Bob.

"Let's round this stock up and head back to Texas."

"Ahh, Mary, we've found some gold and there's probably more," smiled Big Bob.

"That one cursed nugget is probably all the gold in the Indian Territory," retorted Mary.

"No ma'am," laughed Pancho. He held up his gold nugget ring and said, "There's not one, but two."

"What say we give this gold expedition another week without a nugget and then we'll be going back to Texas?" Mary asked.

"Right, guys?" asked Big Bob.

"Yeah, this gold-prospecting is hard work without much reward," Lee Roy popped off.

"Well, men, if there's any more gold in this river the rain will have loosened it up," explained Mac.

"You think so?" asked Lee Roy.

"Shore do, after the river goes back down we'll find gold, or like Mary says, 'We'll be going back to Texas,'" quoted Mac.

That evening, Big Bob sat beside the river watching the swollen river go down. He figured by tomorrow morning the river would be back to normal. The others had rounded up the mules and horses. Only one horse had been spooked bad enough to run into a crevice and it broke its leg. Emanuel had found it and put it out of its misery. The sod roof had been repaired; the gate rebuilt.

A few leaves fell from the scarlet maples that abounded in these woods. They served to remind Big Bob that autumn was drawing to an end. He needed to get Mary down out of these mountains before winter set in.

Their supplies were holding out pretty good, but forty mules ate quite a bit. Running loose had been good for them as they could forage for themselves. The sun was going down as Big Bob took a last look at the river. The golden rays of sunshine bouncing around clouds, pine trees, river water, and the rocky banks, painted a picture that would only be seen once as the circumstances would never be the same again.

THIRTEEN

It was a determined bunch that sat down to breakfast the next morning. Going back to Texas empty-handed was going to be hard for them to accept. Emanuel's eyes were bloodshot, as last night had been his turn on guard duty.

Mac spoke first. "That old river churned its bottom up for us. We should find color today."

"Where's the best areas?" asked Big Bob.

"Well, I'm gonna say the discovery hole and the cabin pool ought to be the most likely."

"Well, I know Pancho wants first shot at the discovery hole," teased Big Bob.

"*Sí señor*," replied Pancho.

I guess Samuel and Cruz will be your panning pardners for the day," said Big Bob. "Ah, Mac, you, me, and Lee Roy get the cabin pool."

"*Señor* Big Bob, if we find gold, I'm gonna fire my pistol three times," Pancho said with a smile.

"Well, you know, this is Indian Territory."

"But we haven't seen any," responded Pancho.

"What do you think Mac?" asked Big Bob.

"After this storm they're probably close to their villages," answered Mac.

"OK, then three shots means gold!" replied Big Bob.

With that last thought, the men took their gold pans and headed for their respective areas. Samuel, Pancho, and Cruz went west down the river till they came to the place where they'd found the nugget earlier. Mac, Lee Roy, and Big Bob went to the cabin pool.

"Darn sight more sand here than what I thought there'd be," observed Lee Roy.

"Yeah, well, after the river went down whatever's in these mountains will show up," explained Mac.

"Well, let's get to it. I can't wait to be rich. My son's gonna need plenty of money for land and cattle," dreamed Big Bob.

"My son?" asked Lee Roy and Mac in unison.

"Yeah, I been meaning to tell ya, Mary's in the family way."

"Well, congratulations, papa," Lee Roy said, smiling.

"That explains why Mary's been wanting to get out of these mountains," sighed Mac.

"Yeah, she's a little itchy to have her own place," said Big Bob.

"You know, if we don't see color today there probably ain't no larger deposit of ore around here. Just some freak of nature that yields a nugget once in a blue moon," said Mac as he took his pan and began to work some sand.

Big Bob and Lee Roy took their pans and began to work in earnest. Mac was on the east end of the sand, while Big Bob was in the middle. Lee Roy worked his way toward Big Bob. At the discovery hole, Samuel and Pancho were working with the real enthusiasm that comes with having found gold there before. By noon, however, they hadn't found a grain of gold. Cruz became discouraged.

"I think I'll go get some of Mary's coffee and see if they've found anything at the cabin pool," Cruz said as he laid down his pan and stretched his legs.

"*Sí Señor* Cruz," Pancho said as he also threw his pan down. "Coffee sounds good to me also."

"Maybe Mary will have some stew ready by now," commented Samuel as he, too, stood up and started for camp.

Mary had seasoned the stew earlier and was tasting it with a spoon when she was surprised by Mac, Lee Roy and Big Bob walking toward the campfire outside the cabin.

"What's the matter, Big Bob?" she asked.

"No color, not even a grain," answered Big Bob.

I can't figure it out," Mac said as he helped himself to a cup of coffee. "Find a nugget as large as a marble, but can't find a single grain."

"Mary, is the stew about done?" asked Lee Roy.

"Done enough. Here, let me hand you a bowl."

"Thanks," was all Lee Roy could say as he sat down and leaned against a pine tree.

"Yonder comes Cruz, they don't look very happy," said Big Bob as he accepted a bowl of stew from Mary.

"Y'all have any luck?" asked Mac as Cruz, Pancho, and Samuel draw near.

"No, *Señor* Mac, none at all," said Cruz as he helped himself to a cup of coffee and a bowl of stew.

"Big Bob, where we gonna spend all this gold we've found?" asked Mary in a sarcastic way.

"Well, I don't rightly know, honey. Maybe we'll have a couple rounds of beer at the first saloon we come to," answered Big Bob.

"We going somewhere where there's a saloon?" asked Mary.

"Yeah, I think after lunch we'll pan one more time, and if we don't find anything, we'll leave for civilization tomorrow," answered Big Bob. "Is that agreeable with everyone?"

"*Sí señor*. Yeah, Big Bob," they said in unison.

"One more shot this afternoon, then we're gone. That's fair enough," said Mac.

"Mary, why don't you start packing your dry goods, and in the morning, all we'll have to do is pack the mules and hit the trail for home," Big Bob said.

"Shore thang, honey," cooed Mary.

"Mary, could I have some leftover stew for ole Popcorn?" asked Cruz as he handed his empty bowl to her.

"Sure," said Mary as she ladled him some meat off the top, as that was the rooster's favorite.

Cruz walked around the side of the cabin where Popcorn's scratch pen was kept. Normally, once or twice a day, Cruz had taken Popcorn table scraps, where the rooster and his hens would enjoy them. Now as Cruz rounded the corner of the cabin, all he could see were the hens that Standish had given him. Popcorn was nowhere in sight. Fearing that the rooster might run into a varmint, he couldn't handle it. Cruz went back to the campfire and told the others what had happened.

"Good hunting, *Señor* Cruz," Pancho wished him as he got up from the campfire and started back toward the discovery hole with Samuel.

The others also got up and went to the cabin pool.

Cruz went back to the scratch pen from which Popcorn had escaped. There he found some tracks, and he followed them into the corral where the rooster had stopped to scratch a pile of mule dung. Following his tracks, they became fewer and further apart, as the ground became rocky. The rooster was heading in a northerly direction toward the river, however, and Cruz decided to stop and listen. Sooner or later that ornery rooster would crow, and Cruz would know where he was.

While he was listening, he could hear Mac and Lee Roy talking as they panned for gold.

"I'm ready to head out of here right now," stated Lee Roy as he threw his last pan of sand into the river.

"Well, I'd like to stay another day or two just trying to figure out where that nugget Pancho found came from. But then again, I might never figure it out. Gold's a funny thing, the harder you look, the harder it is to find," Mac said as he dumped an empty pan.

"Well, you may be right Mac, but winter's just around the corner. Plus, we haven't seen any Indians, but we are trespassing on their land," Big Bob said as he emptied his pan.

"Shore, you're right," agreed Lee Roy as he caught movement behind some poison sumac. Pointing his finger, both Big Bob and Mac placed their hands on their revolvers. About then they were startled to hear, "Ert, ert, err, errrr," as Popcorn crowed.

"It's a good thing he crowed when he did, otherwise he might be in the stew pot for supper," laughed Lee Roy.

"Always wanting to eat my rooster," said Cruz as he emerged from the brush.

Skirting the sand, he climbed over some rocks thickly covered with brush and lots of sumac intertwined with each other. He could see Popcorn strutting behind the sumac. As Cruz worked his way through the natural barrier, he saw Popcorn's head go down into a crevice and emerge with what looked like a kernel of corn. Popcorn shook his head and threw this kernel to one side. Cruz was now close enough to catch Popcorn. Popcorn knew Cruz and offered little resistance.

Cruz had his rooster in his arms and began to turn back through the brush the way he came, when he saw the object Popcorn spit out. Reaching down with his free hand, Cruz picked up a corn-sized nugget of pure gold.

"*Señor* Big Bob, *Señor* Mac, *Señor* Lee Roy, come here. I have something to show you," teased Cruz.

"What's this something?" asked Big Bob.

"Gold!" answered Cruz.

The three men wasted no time finding their way through the sumac.

Mac took the nugget out of Cruz's hand. "Yep, it's solid gold."

"Where did it come from?" asked Big Bob.

"I seen Popcorn's head go down into this crack and come out with it," answered Cruz.

Lee Roy knelt down by the crack and ran his hand into it. He felt around, then pulled it back out with fifteen nuggets the size of corn kernels.

"Hot-diggity-damn!" hollered Mac. A natural cache of gold."

"Yee haw!" hollered Big Bob as he pulled his revolver and fired three shots into the air.

"Wait till Mary and the others see this!" shouted Lee Roy.

"How much do you reckon is in there?" Big Bob asked Mac.

"Well, it's hard to say without breaking off this ridge," Mac said as he pointed along the crack.

"We'll need the picks and hammers," said Big Bob as he rubbed his chin.

Mary and Emanuel came running to the river's edge, then climb around the brush to where the others were. "What's all the shooting about?" asked Mary. "Mary, honey, we've found it! A natural cache of gold nuggets!" answered Big Bob.

"How big a cache?" she asked.

"We don't know," answered Big Bob, then he added, "As soon as Pancho and Samuel get here, we're going to get some picks and hammers to crack this ridge and see just how much there is."

"Mary's hands are small," observed Mac.

"Yeah, Mary, come here and see if you can pull out more gold nuggets than I did!" Lee Roy said as he showed her the gold nuggets in his hand.

"Oh boy!" exclaimed Mary as she eyed the gold nuggets, then positioned herself above the crack. Reaching into the crack, she pulled out a large handful of nuggets. "I'm rich! I'm rich!" hollered Mary as she danced a jig.

"Who's rich?" asked Pancho and Samuel as they stood watching. They had slipped up unobserved as Mary had gotten her first handful of nuggets.

"I'm rich, you're rich, we're all rich!" Mary said deliriously as she danced over to where Pancho and Samuel stood and handed them her nuggets.

"Pure solid gold nuggets!" Pancho said as he looked with wide eyes at Samuel.

Mary was back at the crack, pulling out yet another

handful of gold. Mac had his hat off and offered it to Mary. She promptly placed the gold nuggets in his hat. The men stared in amazement as Mary filled his Stetson in a matter of minutes.

"Next," smiled Mac as he moved out of Big Bob's way. Mary soon had Big Bob's hat full also. Lee Roy stood in line next. Mary had been digging nuggets at a breakneck pace. She stopped to catch her breath.

"Are we tired already?" asked Lee Roy.

"I could do this twenty-four hours a day, seven days a week," replied Mary as she resumed her digging.

"What do you think, Mac?" asked Big Bob.

"Well, perhaps we should retrieve as many nuggets as possible by hand, before we crack under this ledge. If there is more, we might dump this gold when we pry the ridge loose."

"Hmmm… well it wouldn't hurt anything to gather as much as we could before we pry the ridge loose," Big Bob thought out loud.

"Pancho, you and Samuel leave yore hats with Mary and that smiling devil," laughed Big Bob as he pointed to Cruz and shook his head. "We'll go get some packs and saddle bags." Big Bob smiled at Mary. "You! Keep digging."

By the time Big Bob and the others returned from the cabin, Mary had filled the other two hats. Big Bob motioned for Lee Roy and Pancho to hold the saddle bags open. Then he poured the gold from their hats into the saddle bags.

"Here's yore hat back."

"Thanks Big Bob, the light was about to blind this poor old mountain man."

"Well, Mac, you might be a mountain man, but you're not poor anymore," smiled Big Bob.

"Hey Big Bob, when you're right, you're right!"

Lee Roy had a hold of the saddle bags. "You know, I'd bet this set of saddle bags weighs a hundred pounds."

"Lemme see," said Emanuel. "*Sí señor*, they'll weigh a hundred or better. I'll go get a mule to haul them to the cabin."

"I believe gold has made Emanuel more energetic," laughed Big Bob as the lazy Mexican headed for the corral.

Mary finished filling the second saddle bag, dusted off her hands, and announced, "That's all the nuggets I can reach, but there's more back in there, 'cause they feel bigger."

"All right, let's get the picks."

The men needed no second urging, as the excitement had them moving like bees. They were back quickly with picks and two hammers.

"Big Bob, you see that fault in the ledge?" asked Mac.

"Yeah, let's concentrate our efforts in that area, men," commanded Big Bob.

They placed their picks and swung their hammers, the ledge broke into four giant pieces. The men moved one piece.

"Look at all this gold!" whispered Mac in awe.

"Yeah, there's more here than at the U.S. mint!" proclaimed Lee Roy.

"*Sí señors*, enough gold to buy all of Mexico," said Cruz.

"Let's move the other rocks," suggested Big Bob.

Cruz, Samuel, and Pancho grabbed one piece, and Lee Roy, Big Bob, and Mac grabbed another.

"Heave, ho!" the six men shouted together. They all grabbed the last rock together. "Heave, ho!" they shouted in unison again.

"I've heard of huge gold caches before, but this is the largest I've ever seen!" Mac said as he looked from one end to another at the river of gold that stretched before him.

"We're not rich—we're filthy rich!" hollered Mary as she saw what the men had uncovered.

"*Sí señorita*," agreed Pancho, then he asked, "How are we going to move all this gold?"

"Yeah boss, what are we gonna do?" asked Samuel.

"Well, I think we should load all the saddle bags and packs on a couple of the mules and bring them over here."

"No sooner said than done," said Lee Roy, Samuel, and Cruz, still holding Popcorn. Mary had held him while Cruz helped break and move the rocks.

"When this gold-finding rooster is in his scratch pen, I'm gonna shovel me enough gold to build the finest gamecock ranch in the state of Texas," proclaimed Cruz as he approaches the cabin.

"Yeah, let's get a couple of shovels, too," suggested Lee Roy as Samuel caught two of the gentler mules. Cruz had placed Popcorn in his pen and came 'round the cabin with his arms full of saddle bags. After loading them on the mules, Lee Roy headed after another load. In no time at all, they had forty empty saddle bags and packs loaded on the two mules. Samuel and Cruz led the mules to where Big Bob and the others were standing in a guardlike stance over the gold.

"That didn't take y'all too long, but we've only got about three hours of good daylight left," informed Big Bob.

"Well," said Mac, "I don't believe it's going to take too long to load our saddle bags and packs. I believe there's more loose gold here than we can haul."

"Ain't but one way to find out," suggested Lee Roy as he crawled down into the cache. "Hand me a shovel."

Cruz handed him a shovel, then crawled into the other end with a shovel in his hand. Big Bob and Samuel held the flaps on the saddle bags open as the sound of shovels loaded with gold began to fill the air.

In a matter of minutes, the bags were full. Big Bob laid a full saddle bag to one side as he grabbed another empty one. Mac loaded the full saddle bag on the mule's back. Samuel loaded another on the same mule, as they were only going to the cabin and two saddle bags of gold would not tire a mule in that distance.

Mary waved to the men as she led the first mule to the cabin. Emanuel held the second mule while Big Bob and Samuel loaded it also. While Mary waited at the cabin she added some fire wood to the forgotten pot of stew. Emanuel soon arrived and unloaded the gold from the mules and carried it into the cabin.

"I never thought we'd find this gold," Mary said as she stirred the stew and Emanuel passed by carrying a saddle bag of gold.

"Me neither, Miss Mary," said Emanuel, shaking his head. "It's a dream come true."

Emanuel took the two mules back by himself as Mary tended the cooking and guarded the gold. Chopping some stew meat, she headed around the cabin to Popcorn's scratch pen and said, "Popcorn, you're the greatest. You help us cross the river and find the gold for us poor ole humans. Here's a snack for you." With that, Mary threw the chopped meat to the strutting cock.

The men, meanwhile, were loading the gold as fast as they could. Ten trips with the two mules double-loaded, and all their saddle bags and packs were full. The men could not resist as they filled their pockets with nuggets, also.

"There is still some gold in the cache," observed Big Bob.

"Yeah, there is, but we can't haul it without substituting gold for supplies. Besides, we have enough gold for two lifetimes," remarked Mac.

"Let's get a good night's sleep and head home for Texas," remarked Lee Roy.

"*Sí señor*, that's the best idea I've heard. I can smell Mary's stew from here," said Samuel.

"*Sí amigos*, this gold digging has me very, very, hungry," Cruz said as he licked his lips.

The weary gold diggers headed for the cabin. No one noticed the Indian on the east side of the canyon, who had observed their actions for the past hour. Turning and heading in a northerly direction, he found the camp where ten of his comrades were cooking a deer over the open campfire.

FOURTEEN

"Lone Wolf, what troubles you so?" asked the chief.

"The white-eyes have come into our hunting grounds and found the yellow metal they call gold," Lone Wolf spoke angrily.

"They must be punished!" said the chief, as he brandished his ceremonial spear and plunged it into the ground.

"How will we punish them?" asked Rattlesnake Fang as he carved another piece off the carcass roasting over the campfire.

"Torture and death," spoke the chief in a voice of finality.

Not knowing of the Indian's presence, Big Bob and the others were feasting on Mary's stew, planning the next day's journey.

"We'll follow the Kiamichi a couple miles, then cut through the forest south to mountain Fork," suggested Mac to the others.

Big Bob and the others nodded their heads in agreement. After supper while they were still gathered around the split log table, Mac produced a half-full bottle of whiskey.

"Everyone hold out your cups," commanded Mac. Giving each one a small drink, Mac announced a toast. "Here's to the luckiest, richest friends I will ever have."

"And here's to you, Mac," replied the others as the cups clinked together.

"Oh, Mac, I have a question for you." said Mary.

"What is it, Mary?"

"I've heard what the others are going to buy with their gold, but I've never heard what you're going to do," asked Mary.

"Well, Mary," Mac said in an serious tone, "I'm gonna build the biggest distillery in Texas."

"Why?" asked Mary.

"Because I know five cowhands that just became million-aires and will want an unending flow of whiskey."

Everyone laughed at this statement.

"This millionaire has a long dangerous journey ahead of him tomorrow and needs his sleep. What say we all turn in?" Big Bob said as he headed for the kerosene lamp. The men were give out and readily agreed.

The next morning the men were excited as they loaded the mules down with gold. Finally every mule was loaded and every horse was saddled. Mary was the last one out of their makeshift cabin.

"I'm gonna miss this place," Mary said as she pulled the door shut for the last time.

"Me too," said Big Bob as he beckoned Mary to her horse.

Mac led the way, with six mules on lead ropes behind him. Cruz was behind Mac, also with six mules. The rest were leading mules. Big Bob brought up the rear with Mary ahead of him. They were a mile and a half down the Kiamichi River when Mac saw the tracks of unshod ponies in the river sand. Easing the mules alongside the riverbank, Mac dismounted for a closer inspection.

"What's the matter?" asked Cruz as he pulled up. "Indian pony tracks," stated Mac.

"How fresh are the tracks?" asked Cruz.

"Not over a day old," replied Mac.

Samuel, Pancho, Lee Roy, Emanuel, and Big Bob wondered what the hold up was. Big Bob finally gave the ropes for his mules to Mary, then rode up to the front of the line. As he rode to the front of the line, he caught a movement out of the corner of his eye on the north bank. Shifting his eyes slowly, he spied an Indian on a horse, moving westward. He rode on to where Mac was still examining the pony tracks.

"How many are there?" asked Big Bob as he stopped a few feet from Mac.

"Look's like about ten or eleven."

"We need to find a place to defend ourselves and quick!" said Big Bob.

"How come?" asked Mac.

"I've seen one on the north bank, and he's covered with war paint."

"You remember the waterfall and the secret cave?" suggested Cruz.

"Yeah," responded Big Bob. "Why don't you take over the lead and I'll go back to the rear with Mary."

After Big Bob had left, Mac asked Cruz, "Is the place y'all are talking about easily defended?"

"It's a natural fort, if we can beat the Indians to it," replied Cruz as he headed down the river.

Crossing over some steep boulders, Cruz emerged into a roomlike area with a wall-like rock on three sides. In front of the room were scattered boulders, offering protection for defenders. As they entered this protective zone, the Indians realized what they were up to and opened fire on Big Bob, who was at the rear and caught in the open.

One of their bullets killed a mule with Popcorn on it. Popcorn's tether broke when the mule hit the ground and he escaped into the woods. The hen's fate was sealed when the fallen mule smashed them to death.

Two of the Indians made the mistake of showing them-selves as targets, and Big Bob nailed them both through the heart. The Indians backed off after seeing such shooting.

Cruz thought fast, "Their isn't enough room for us and the mules in here. Strip the saddle bags off them and run them on through," he commanded.

Mac saw the hopelessness of keeping the mules and obeyed. Stripping the packs and bags off his mules, he made room for the others as they arrived.

Emanuel was ahead of Mary as he broke over the pass, leading his mules into the rock shelter. A shot rang out and he fell forward into his saddle as he died. Mac caught Emanuel's horse by its bridle as he fell out of his saddle.

"He's dead," announced Mac after a quick look. "Get his packs and move those mules out of here."

Samuel and Pancho moved quickly, making room for Big Bob and Mary, as Cruz wisely guarded the exit. Mac moved toward the entrance to guard Big Bob's and Mary's arrival. Suddenly an Indian with a tomahawk jumped from a boulder toward Mary as she entered the shelter. Big Bob and Mac fired simultaneously, killing the red man instantly. Big Bob waited nervously as Mary's mules were the next to be stripped and herded out the exit.

Just as Big Bob entered the pass going to the shelter, two Indians rose from the boulder next to the entrance and opened fire. In the hail of bullets, Big Bob's horse was shot out from under him. He jumped clear of his mount and returned fire. Mac also had his pistol out and shot one of the Indians in the head. The other Indian moved to the other side of the boulder, offering Big Bob a clean shot. As Big Bob shot, the dying Indian shot his rifle from the hip and hit Big Bob in the chest. Mac ran to Big Bob's side.

"Tell Mary I love her." Those were his last words.

"Shore, Big Bob," Mac promised as Big Bob died in his arms.

"Is he hurt bad?" asked Mary as she ran up to Mac's side.

"He said, 'Tell Mary I love her,'" Mac said as he looked into Mary's eyes.

"Oh no!" cried Mary as she started sobbing uncontrollably.

Mac dragged Big Bob's body into the shelter and laid it next to Emanuel. They stripped the packs off Big Bob's mules and laid his gold in the corner with the rest.

Mary was on the verge of being hysterical. Mac walked her over to where the saddle bags were stacked, comforting her as much as possible before he resumed his place among the others. Lee Roy and Pancho guarded the entrance, while Cruz and Samuel were guarding the rear.

"Why don't they attack?" Lee Roy asked Pancho.

"I don't know *señor*," Pancho said as he shook his head.

"They hurt us, but we hurt 'em worse," volunteered Mac. "There weren't but eleven Indian ponies when I crossed their trail."

"Counting the last one Big Bob shot, that leaves only five or six in their party," said Lee Roy.

"That's enough to keep us from making it to a place of safety. Besides, we're on their stomping grounds," Mac thought out loud.

"It may be stomping grounds, but I know a waterfall with a underground passage to that boulder over yonder." Cruz pointed with his rifle.

"Do you think you can make it to there unobserved and take a look-see?" asked Mac.

"Sure, I can. I'm gonna leave my rifle here and take only my knife and pistol," replied Cruz.

"Good luck, *señor*," said Pancho as Cruz slipped through the boulders toward the waterfall.

Cruz worked his way down from the roomlike rock until he could see the released mules eating bluestem between the boulders. They were not disturbed by his appearance as they would have been if they had spotted a stranger. So Cruz felt fairly certain that no Indians were in his immediate area.

Approaching the waterfall, Cruz drew his revolver and placed his hat over it to keep it dry. Stepping quickly through the water and into the darkness, he placed the pistol back into his holster.

Feeling his way over the once-traveled passage, he found his way to the shaft that led upward. Climbing ever so quietly, he finally emerged between the boulders that marked the entrance to the shaft. He wanted to suck in a big lungful of air after the exhausting climb, but was afraid an Indian might hear him.

He slowly recovered from the climb and eased around the boulders to see how far west the sun had traveled. It had been early morning at the time of the attack, now it was nearing sundown. The boulders had long shadows. Perhaps he would be harder to see if he moved into one of the shadows away from the shaft. As he moved toward the boulder, he saw a feather move.

Reaching for his fighting knife, he was ready to defend himself when the Indian stepped around the boulder. Almost coming face to face, the Indian drew his knife as Cruz stabbed the red man in his left arm. Jerking his left arm free, the Indian kicked Cruz in his right leg, throwing him off balance and gaining temporary freedom.

They circled each other warily, then Cruz grabbed the Indian by the wounded arm and pulled him toward him, plunging his knife into the Indian's chest. The Indian was taken by surprise as the knife entered his body, but simply twitched his body to prevent the knife from doing any more damage. With his wounded arm, he grabbed Cruz by his shirt and thrust his weapon into Cruz's belly, burying his knife to the hilt. Cruz, upon feeling the pain, went into a frenzied fury and pulled his knife out of the Indian's body and stabbed the red man repeatedly with it.

The Indian died and slid to the ground. Cruz, knowing he was hurt, took a quick look around the countryside anyway. Seeing no pressing danger, he grabbed the dead red man and threw his body into the shaft heading to the underground passage. Looking at the blood spots upon the rocks, he picked up a handful of dirt and covered them. Walking rock to rock, he hid his trail to the shaft and eased his way to the underground passage. He walked through the passage and into the refreshing waterfall.

"I haven't heard anything other than a hoot owl this evening!" Mac said as he looked around the darkened country.

"Indians don't attack in the dark, " Lee Roy said, after hesitating. "Do they?"

"No, " Mac said. "No warrior will go to the happy hunting ground if he dies in the dark."

"Shhh!" Pancho gave the sign for quiet. Something was moving in the dark toward them.

"Don't shoot," came the whispered command. Cruz came into camp slowly.

"He is hurt." Those were the first words Mary had said since Big Bob's death.

"Bring him to me," Mary said as she placed a couple saddle blankets on the ground to make a bed.

"Take off his shirt," she ordered.

"What happened, Cruz?" asked Mac.

"Indian on top of the shaft by two boulders," answered Cruz. "I killed him and threw his body down the shaft."

"Yeah, but he gave you a nasty wound," consoled Lee Roy.

"I'll live."

"I don't know. If we had any medicine you might," put in Mary, after examining his wound.

"I've got some whiskey saved back just for this kind of thing," Mac said as he went for his jug. When he got back, Mary held Cruz's stomach skin apart and Mac poured the whiskey on the wound.

"I know this hurts," Mac said after he was done. "Here, now take a drink." Cruz readily accepted the drink.

"You know with Cruz killing that Indian it leaves only four Indians out there," Lee Roy said as he gestured to the night.

"Yeah, only four Indians," said Pancho as he moved back to a guard position after seeing Cruz doctored.

FIFTEEN

Lone Wolf sat despondently staring across the campfire at Chief Eagle Feather.

"These white-eyes are good," said Black Hat.

"I will kill them all," muttered Lone Wolf.

"Yes, I agree on killing them all. They have killed our brothers, and Duck, our best scout, has disappeared," Chief Eagle Feather spoke slowly, as if he were thinking out loud. "We are no match when it comes to rifles. They have fired six shots and killed six warriors. No one heard a shot when Duck disappeared. He may be alive, but if he were he would be here now."

The chief rose from where he was sitting to address his three remaining warriors. "We must sheath our rifles and stalk the white-eyes in the old way. Knife, bow, arrow, cunning as only the brave warrior knows. We will not attack, but remain in the woods and watch them from afar. When they no longer see or hear us they will believe we are gone. We will catch them away from their group and quietly kill one. When another comes looking, we will kill him, only the twang of the bows shall be heard."

Lone Wolf nodded his head. "It is easy to see why they call you chief."

The sun came up the next morning as it can do only in the mountains, rays shooting through the pine trees, bouncing off the foliage and boulders. For all its beauty, it could not cheer up Mary, for she had lost the one she loved. Samuel and Mac had dug two graves during the night. They wrapped the bodies in blankets and placed them in the ground.

Mac took off his hat. "Big Bob was a good horseman, cattleman, and true friend."

Lee Roy cleared his throat and said, "A better shot and natural leader I never knew."

Mary was sobbing. "I love you, Big Bob. Good-bye."

Pancho twisted his hat. "Emanuel was a good helper and true friend.

Samuel simply nodded his head.

Cruz said, *"Adios amigos,"* then turned his head as the tears welled up in his eyes.

The others walked over to the campfire while Pancho and Lee Roy buried their friends. Pancho had put on a pot of coffee before the burial, now Mac helped himself to a cup. Samuel rolled a cigarette.

"I could see the saddle bags on the dead mule," Mac said as he took another sip of coffee.

"Yeah, they're still full," Samuel said as he exhaled.

Cruz, who had been listening, said, "The mules we turned loose are scattered in the valley below us grazing and drinking fresh water. They seem undisturbed."

"I don't know what the Indians wanted—other than our scalps," Mac said.

"Do you think they will attack us again?" asked Samuel.

"It's hard to say," Mac replied. "They've taken some heavy losses, and it would be suicide for them to confront us again."

"Ya reckon they've went for help?" asked Lee Roy as he returned from the burying.

"They could have. That would be the smartest move on their part," answered Mac.

"I think the smartest move on our part would be to get some help," said Cruz.

"That's a good idea, Cruz. We could hide the gold in amongst the rocks and hightail it out of here," Mac said.

"I don't think the Indians know about the chimney leading to the secret passage," suggested Cruz.

"That's a natural place all right, but why don't we hide it in one of the cracks where the Indians, or no one else for that matter, can get to it. When we come back we'll bring some dynamite and blow the rocks off the gold," suggested Mac.

"*Sí Señor* Mac, that is a good idea," agreed Samuel.

"What say you and I go look for such a place," Mac said to Samuel.

"*Sí señor*, let's go."

After Mac and Samuel had left, Pancho poured himself a cup of coffee. "*Señor* Cruz, do you think it is wise to heave the gold?"

"The gold would slow us down, and we might not make it away in time. I'd rather be alive and a poor man than a rich dead man."

"*Sí señor*."

Mary, who had been sitting on the saddle bags, came up to the campfire. "May I have a cup of coffee?"

"Sure," Cruz said as he poured her a cup.

"If we're going to leave the gold, we should leave some kind of mark to help us find it," Mary suggested.

"A map, if you will," thought Pancho. "I used to carve headstones in Mexico. I could carve one on a large boulder or wall."

"I don't think the map should be easily deciphered by a casual passerby," said Lee Roy.

"We could make some type of code book," Mary thought out loud. "Made from stone tablets and only one set."

"*Sí señora*, I like it," Cruz agreed.

Samuel and Mac returned. "We've found a suitable place."

"Good," replied Lee Roy. "Pancho is going to carve us a map."

"A map?" asked Mac.

"Sure, that way we can find our gold when we return," Lee Roy pointed to a big boulder in the curve of the creek. "That boulder would be big enough for a map, wouldn't it, Pancho?"

"*Sí señor.*"

"Pancho, let's be the first to hide buried treasure," Mac said as he picked up a set of saddle bags.

"*Sí Señor* Mac," Pancho said as he slung a set of saddle bags upon his shoulders. Samuel grabbed a set of saddle bags and followed them.

When they had gone a hundred feet, Mac threw the saddle bags into a crevice about three feet wide and thirty-five feet deep. Pancho and Samuel did the same. On the way back, they met Lee Roy and Mary, who had also begun to help bury the gold. Mac pointed to the crevice.

"No way anyone can get to this gold," Lee Roy said as he threw his first load to the bottom.

"I know, that's the beauty of using this crevice. No one would ever think of looking in there."

No one would have to look in there if they already knew where the gold was. And that was exactly what the Indians were doing, watching the white men hide their precious yellow metal.

When the last saddle bag was carried from the roomlike area, Mac looked at Lee Roy and said, "One last detail, we need to get that set of saddle bags off that dead mule and into the ground."

"I'm game, let's get Cruz and Samuel to cover us while we make the trip."

"Y'all ready?"

"*Sí amigo.*"

Mac and Lee Roy worked their way from boulder to boulder. They approached the dead animal carefully. Mac stood guard as Lee Roy worked the bags out from under the mule.

"I don't believe the Indians are around," said Mac as he looked around.

"I hope you're right."

Their return to the campfire was uneventful.

"Let's take this last bag of gold with us to buy supplies for our return," suggested Lee Roy as they sat down by the campfire.

"Sounds like a good idea," answered Mac.

"There's enough gold in this one saddle bag to rent the third cavalry if we need them," laughed Lee Roy.

"Yeah, if we get out of here before they return," Mac said dryly, then continued, "Why don't we set up camp down by the big boulder and help Pancho carve the map."

"Yeah, the sooner we're done, the sooner we can hit the trail home."

They rode the remaining mules down to the boulder, saving their horses' strength for the long journey home. Pancho drew a map in the dirt. Everyone liked his ideas.

"I need a couple of marker rocks to make this map."

"Sure," replied Cruz as he took his lariat rope from his saddle. He then measured off three lariat rope lengths to a large boulder.

"How about here," he waved back to Pancho.

"Over a little to the right," Pancho motioned. Cruz nodded, then started carving a wolf's head on the boulder.

Pancho began the map on the big boulder. The first thing he carved on the map was a curved arrow matching the creek's natural bend. He then carved a sheep sitting on top of the arrow. The sheep looked away from the wolf. By then Cruz had finished drawing the wolf's head, which looked at the sheep. Cruz walked slowly back to the sheep rock. His knife wound was beginning to bother him as he moved among the boulders.

"Say, Pancho, could my next carving be a little more simple?"

"Sure, Cruz, just draw me an *X* on that boulder." Pancho pointed at a ninety degree angle from the sheep to the wolf's head line-up. Cruz took the lariat rope and again measured three lengths from the sheep rock.

"Pancho, there is a round melon-sized piece of rock sticking out to one side of this boulder," yelled Cruz as he stood behind the rock.

Pancho glanced back to where Samuel was standing above the gold, then back to where Cruz stood.

"That's a perfect line-up. Go ahead and carve an *X*," Pancho commanded.

While Cruz carved his simple *X*, Pancho placed the waterfall on the map next to the tail of the arrow. By the time the waterfall was completed, Cruz had carved his *X* and returned to the sheep rock. Samuel was called down from where he was standing over the gold. He brought two small flat rocks. Samuel and Cruz began to carve words into the rocks, telling how to interpret the sheep rock.

Mac, Mary, and Lee Roy had begun to cook a pot of fresh stew made from mule meat. The campfire was close enough to the sheep rock to cast an eerie light against the rock as the sun went down.

Pancho took a bowl of stew, needing to give his weary hands a break. Samuel and Cruz also ate a bowl of stew.

"That's a good map," remarked Mac.

"*Muchas gracias, Señor* Mac, I've had to hide a few things in my time, but never this much gold," Pancho explained. "I'll place a turtle's head, rattlesnake's head, and a gate to hell near the gold to guard it when I'm through with the sheep rock."

"I like that idea," said Cruz as he finished his stew and went back to work on his tablets.

"What do you wish for me to do?" Samuel asked Pancho.

"I will draw the formation that comes out of the ground at the end of the arrow for you to finish carving while I go and put signs around the gold," Pancho answered.

"*Sí amigo*," agreed Samuel.

Pancho finished drawing the map for Samuel to carve. He then left with Mac to mark the actual burial site.

"Will we be able to leave in the morning?" Mac asked Pancho as they headed for the burial site.

"*Sí señor*, if we work all night we will be able to ride out of here with the gold well marked," answered Pancho.

"Yes that sounds good, but Cruz is still hurting from the knife fight. Do you think he can stand a hard ride?"

"I don't know how bad he is, but he hurts when he walks. Maybe he will make it; maybe he won't. But he is a tough *señor*, very tough."

"I hope so, Pancho. Look, the moon is coming up."

"Ahh, yes, more than enough light to work by."

Pancho worked past midnight, then smiled as he said, "I'm finished, Mac, let's head back to the others."

When Pancho and Mac returned to camp, they found Samuel finishing the sheep rock while Lee Roy and Mary watched. Cruz had finished the tablets and gone to sleep.

SIXTEEN

Having spent thirty-six hours hiding and mapping the gold, Mac and the others were anxious to get out of the area. Unobserved, the Indians could tell the white men were preparing to leave.

"I think they shall ride between those boulders," Lone Wolf said, pointing to the nearby formation.

"Then we shall conceal ourselves and attack with bow and arrow. You get the first shot," Chief Eagle Feather said, pointing to Lone Wolf.

Mary and the others checked their weapons as they had done every morning. They silently mounted their remaining mules and horses. Mac led the way, with Lee Roy and Pancho following close behind. Mary found herself in the middle, with Samuel and Cruz behind her. They rode carefully as their mounts' hooves made an occasional noise on the granite rock.

They traveled half a mile, when Mac saw two boulders on either side of the trail. Still believing the Indians had returned to their village, he headed between the two large rocks and emerged on the other side. Lee Roy passed the boulders as Lone Wolf raised his bow and shot Mac in the chest! As Mac fell from his saddle, Lee Roy drew his pistol and killed Lone Wolf. Chief Eagle Feather fired his bow and hit Lee Roy in the heart.

Pancho, who had jumped off his horse so he could fight from the ground, fired his pistol and hit the chief above his left ear. Pancho was caught in a cross fire from the two remaining Indians.

Samuel and Mary opened fire, but the two Indians ducked behind cover. Dismounting, they both attacked the Indian on the right. Cruz jumped off his horse, only to open his knife wound again. The pain was so bad, he could hardly move. He hid behind a large rock as his friends disappeared from view.

Not expecting so fast an attack on his position, the warrior was surprised to have two opponents at his throat. He broke free from cover and shot his bow, as Mary and Samuel both fired. Going to the happy hunting ground, the Indian could only smile as he saw Samuel's face freeze in the expression of death.

Not knowing what to do, Mary started back toward Cruz with her pistol cocked. As she crept past a bush, a hand reached out and grabbed the wrist which held the pistol.

Flipping her to the ground, Black Hat easily disarmed her. Mary's left hand found his knife, and seizing the opportunity, she stabbed him in the right side. Black Hat slapped Mary with the captured revolver, knocking her unconscious. He took the knife from her hand and wiped it on his buckskins. While Mary was out, Black Hat removed her blouse and made a bandage for his knife wound. Looking down at her bare breasts, he pulled her pants and boots off. Smiling, he removed his breechcloth. Placing his body between her legs, he rubbed her head where the revolver struck her.

As Mary came around, Black Hat placed his hand on his knife. Mary groggily stared at Black Hat, then at her nude body, knowing what he had in mind. She started to scream, but his huge hand prevents her from doing so. As he placed the sharp knife against her throat, a trickle of blood ran down her neck.

Calming somewhat, Mary prepared for the worst. Just as Black Hat prepared for penetration, a shot rang out, striking him above his left shoulder blade. Falling forward, he plunged his knife deep into Mary's breast.

Cruz, still unsteady and dizzy from the crash-landing from his horse, managed to reach Mary's side before she died.

"Cruz…you're the only one left," Mary said, blood oozing out of her wound. "Thanks for trying."

"Anytime, Mary, anytime," Cruz cried, tears streaming down his cheeks.

"Good luck…Cruz," was all she said as she died.

"Why, Lord, why?" Cruz asked, gently laying Mary's hand down.

Cruz's horse had walked up beside him and put his head down, with the reins dragging. Cruz arose slowly, catching the horse by the mane and patting his neck. Surveying the corpses around him, he stood with the help of his horse.

"I wish I could bury each and every one, but I'm sick, and time is important to my survival," Cruz said, apologizing to the dead. He took off his hat and offered this prayer: "Dear Lord, these were good, God-fearing people who were friends to the end."

Cruz then mounted his horse and rode away toward Big Cedar.

Cruz's knife wound turned nasty as he rode day and night. Sometimes he would sleep in the saddle, as his horse cropped a few bites of premium bluestem. The only time he would dismount would be for water, which he used to clean his wound.

Cruz had nearly made it to Big Cedar when gangrene set

in his wound. He ran across some settlers, who sent for a doctor. They were by a stream, where the settlers cared for him until the doctor came.

The doctor arrived and eased Cruz's pain. When they loaded him into the doctor's wagon, he was dizzy and disoriented. He asked the doctor to stop the wagon, which he did. Coming back to Cruz, he was told to look in his saddle bags, which the settlers had loaded.

Looking inside them, the doctor pulled out the Spanish plaque. Cruz attempted to tell the doctor where the sheep rock was, but he was too ill. He managed to tell him about the gold, then gave him the plaque to pay his bill and died.